Somet

to

Talk About

&

Other Stories

Kenneth Spencer Jr.

This is a work of fiction. Names, characters, businesses, events, and incidents are the product of the author's imagination. Any resemblance to actual persons, living or dead, or actual events is purely coincidental.

© Kenneth Spencer Jr. 2020

First printed in Great Britain by Kenneth Spencer, Jr. 2020

For Cherissie, Rachel, and Huy

Acknowledgment

I would like to say a big thank you to Vanessa Chivers, who helped me whip these stories into shape.

Contents

Broken

❧

Billy Washington sat back in his computer chair and sighed heavily, letting out a long slow breath. He had given up trying to turn on the computer for the umpteenth time in the last five minutes. It was broken, and there was no denying it. It was broken and Billy was pissed. There'd be no Twitter or Facebook and the biggest bummer of all, there'd be no Sasha Grey. Not that he would have needed Sasha Grey if he still had Natasha.

Natasha Gordon was the most amazing girl he'd ever met and the prettiest one he'd ever dated. For the six months they had dated, he had been walking on air, until one day he hit the ground again, hard.

One evening while they were out enjoying a milkshake at a 1950s retro diner, after taking a sip of her strawberry milkshake she looked up at him. She said it as simply as though she had asked how his day was or how his new book was coming along.

'Billy, I don't think we should see each other anymore.'

Suddenly the red chairs and white walls became a blurred pink as the room began to spin. Billy felt as though he was riding the hearts and diamonds at the fairground. When the room stopped spinning, the seat in front of him was empty. He sat there for a good while not listening to the golden oldies floating from the juke box, just replaying the last words that the best woman he'd ever known had said to him.

'I don't think we should see each other anymore.'

For the past six months, he replayed that phrase over and over in his head, hoping that she would rethink it and come back to him. He checked her Facebook and Twitter pages almost daily, for a hint or a sign that she was thinking of him. Maybe she would put up a quote or a picture that they shared together. However, over the last six months, there hadn't been anything. There were lots of pictures, posts, and tweets, but nothing that gave him the glimmer of hope he'd been looking for. Now that this stupid thing was broken, he couldn't even do that.

Billy had tried everything to get the computer working again. He took out the plugs from the mains and waited a few minutes before putting them back in and then tried turning it back on. Nothing. At the recommendation of his best friend, Huy, Billy removed the cover of his tower and carefully removed all the dust with the hose of a vacuum cleaner. He pressed the power button again and still nothing.

Billy drummed his fingers on the desk and then reached for his phone and called the last number dialled. He put the phone to his ear and waited for an answer.

"Sup dude, did it work?'

'Nope, nothing.'

'I'm gonna have to come over and take a look at it then, but I can't do that 'til the weekend,' Huy said.

'That's okay. I can hold out 'til then. I still got the telly and a shit load of movies to watch. That should keep me going 'til you get here.' Maybe this is a good thing. It gives me a good excuse when my agent calls asking me how far along I am with the new novel. I can then give her the reason, 'Not far at all because my computer conked out.'

'And how far along are you with the new novel? I hope you saved it on a USB because if the computer is dead, you might have to start all over again,' Huy said, with worry in his voice.

'I haven't written a word.'

'No way, dude! Why the hell not?'

'I haven't written anything since Natasha—'

'Oh, please don't start with her again. I'm surprised that you wrote anything while you were stuck up her arse. Too busy trying to keep her happy.'

'I was not. But she was the best girl I ever had. She was my muse—'

'If she was your muse, you would have written something. You would have been turning stories out as big and fast as Stephen King, instead of looking starry-eyed at everything she said and did.'

'She was the most amazing girl I ever met and—'

'Wait there one second. As your best mate, I'd like to say this. A, love is a two-way street, and B, wait another second while I log onto Amazon and buy you a pair of balls, as yours seems to have fallen off,' Huy said, with mock seriousness.

'This is no joke, Huy. Maybe my first book was a fluke. It seems like I have nothing to say anymore.'

'That's because you've been cooped up in that house, moping over a girl who doesn't want you anymore. Look, get back to taking those long walks you used to take.'

'Yeah, but every route I used to take with Natasha.'

'Find another route and rediscover the pen and paper and go sit in a café. Lots of writers write in cafés, don't they? Listen, I have to go. I'm almost at work. But I'll check in with you on Friday,' Huy said.

'Okay, see you and thanks.'

'And remember to get out of that house for once. I'll bet you some inspiration will hit you at some point, and you'll find something to write about. You still have something to say. I'm sure you have a couple of good ones in you yet. You just need to forget that silly woman and get on with it,' Huy said laughing. 'Later, dude.'

'See you,' Billy said, laughing for the first time that morning.

*

When billionaire businessman, Dean Grey, is found dead in his study, Detective Philip Cain is put on the case. When Cain gets back to the station from the crime scene, an old friend is waiting for him, who confesses to the murder. After hearing his friend's confession, Cain has no choice but to arrest his old school chum. But Cain hasn't even finished writing the first line of his report when another man he knew comes in and also confesses to the killing. With both men giving information only the killer would know, they take Detective Cain on a ride of lust, greed, and murder.

'The best crime novel this decade.'
Bert Thompson, *The Gazette*

'A gripping page-turner. A great debut.'
Heather Wright, *Daily News*

'Smart, sexy, and cool. An intense debut thriller.'
Carl Peterson, Storytelling.com

More like a third-rate Harper Lee, but at least she most likely chose not to write another book, unlike myself who just can't think of anything, Billy thought. He stood in the crime section of his local bookstore, holding a copy of *Killing Mr. Grey*, his debut novel. Billy crouched down and slid it back into its slot with all the W's and stood back up. It annoyed him to see that he only had one title on display, whereas all the other authors had several.

He walked over to the stationary section where he picked up a red leather-bound notebook and a gel-grip roller pen and took them to the counter.

Great, cut me open and pour salt on it, why don't you, Billy thought, as he got to the counter and saw the man behind it reading Stephen King's *Misery*.

'Hello, John.'

'Hi, Billy, how's it going?' John asked him as he put the book down and stood up.

'I'm good, John. How are you?'

'Can't complain. Well I could, I own an independent bookstore, for Christ's sake. Believe me, I could. Sometimes I think it would be better to just shut up my shop and go work for one. But then I remember I did that, and at least now I own my own shop. If a customer comes and gets rude, at least...' John glanced to his left and right to make sure there were no kids present. '...I can tell them to fuck off,' John said quietly.

'True.' Billy said, nodding.

'And that in itself must be rewarding. But all the other stuff that comes with the store causes you to get one of those,' Billy said, pointing to John's hairless head.

'That's cool. At least you don't need to worry about the barber. I hate having to go and sit in one chair for an hour only then to sit in another.'

'Being thirty-five and bald is no joke. I liked my hair. Anyway, how is the new book coming along? It's been a while.'

'Don't remind me. I'm trying, and nothing is coming,' Billy said, rolling his eyes.

'It will come. Just give it time.'

'Thanks. Can I get these?' Billy asked, placing the notebook on the counter and changing the subject.

John picked the notebook up and flipped it over so that he could see the price sticker.

'That's sixteen ninety-nine,' John said, entering the price into the cash register. Billy took his wallet out and tapped his debit card on the reader.

'You want a bag?'

'No thanks, John. It was nice speaking to you.'

'You too. Good luck with the new book. When it's finished maybe we can do a reading or a Q&A one evening,' John said happily.

'If it gets done, I'd love that. Have a good day, John. See you soon.'

'You too,' John said, smiling as he sat back down in his chair and picked up his book.

Billy left the bookshop and walked down the street. He stopped as he felt something wet fall on his head. As he continued down the street, the heavens opened up as a light, but steady, rain began to fall.

'Fuck,' Billy mumbled as he turned on to Church Street. He didn't have an umbrella with him or a hood on his jacket.

Billy turned into the first café he saw. He stood in the doorway for a moment, watching the scene before him, which resembled something from the floor of the stock market. Too many people, too much noise, and nowhere to sit, let alone think. Billy let the door slowly close as he left, shutting out the noise as the door clicked shut. Billy watched the scene inside the café for a moment longer and then continued walking down the street, trying to avoid the onslaught of people with their umbrellas up. Billy bobbed and weaved his way through the umbrellas. He stopped when he reached another café.

Peering through the window, he saw only three people scattered about at tables. As he pushed open the door and stepped inside, the only noise he heard was coming from the coffee machine and a classical piece of music coming from the speakers behind the counter. The café itself wasn't much to look at; not like the posh contemporary one he had passed on. This café was a 'builders café.' It had eight tables for four people; four on each side of the café, a glass chiller display filled with sandwich fillings, and behind that, a grill, a fridge, and a coffee machine.

Billy walked up to the counter where a tired-looking plump woman in her late forties was wiping down the counter. She stopped as Billy got to the counter and smiled half-heartedly.

'Hi, what can I get ya?'

'Hello. A hot chocolate, please.'

'Sure. That's two-twenty, please,' the woman said, ringing the amount up on the cash register. Billy took his card out of his wallet.

'Sorry, love. It's cash only,' the woman said apologetically. Billy flipped the coin compartment of his wallet, opened and poured the change into his hand, and began counting it out.

'Just about,' Billy said, more to himself than to the

lady, as he gathered together the correct change with just a few pennies to spare. Swiping the change with one hand from the counter and into the other, Billy handed her the money.

'Sorry.'

'It's okay. We're a café. We need the change,' the woman said, as she put the change into the till and prepared his hot chocolate. The woman handed Billy his drink.

'Thanks,' he said cheerfully.

'You're welcome,' the woman said, offering Billy the same half-hearted smile she did when he first walked in. Billy nodded, smiling back at her and turned in search of a seat.

It was the book that first caught his attention. The woman came later. To come across someone reading one of his favourite novels was rare. It's not like it was *Harry Potter* or *The Notebook*. To come across someone reading James M. Cain's *The Postman Always Rings Twice* was rare. Billy walked towards the woman who sat reading at the table by the door.

'Just so you're not disappointed, the postman never does come knocking. Nevertheless, it's a great book.'

'I know,' the woman said without looking up, her nose still stuck in the book.

'Mind if I sit?' Billy asked, putting his cup down on the table. As the cup hit the table, the woman lowered her book and looked up at him.

'Maybe I should get back to work? I mean, with it being so busy and all that our customers have nowhere to sit,' the woman said, staring up at Billy. Billy picked up his cup and looked around, feeling more than a bit awkward.

'It's okay. You can sit down. I'm just messing with you,' the woman said, smiling. Her light-brown eyes danced mischievously, and Billy stood there for a long moment as his breath caught in his throat and his mouth went dry.

'What? Have you changed your mind?' she asked.

Billy sat down, pushing in his chair and placing his items on the table.

'I'm—' Billy began.

'William Washington. I'm Eva,' the woman said, cutting him off.

'You know who I am?' Billy asked, genuinely surprised.

'Of course. You wrote *Killing Mr. Grey*. The best-selling novel of 2016.'

'It wasn't the best.'

'Well, one of the biggest. According to what it states on the cover of your paperback editions, you've sold three million copies worldwide,' Eva said, folding the corner of her page, and putting her book aside.

'Everyone has one good story in them. It's having a second and maybe even a third that counts,' he said drily.

'Are you working on anything of late?' Eva asked, biting into her muffin.

'It would seem that I have only the one. I feel like Vanilla Ice or MC Hammer. Hell, they may be remembered for only one hit, but at least they had other songs that made the charts. I only have one book. I was thinking earlier today that I'm a third-rate Harper Lee and even she wrote more than one book.'

'*Go Set a Watchman* was just a cash grab if you ask me,' Eva said.

'That may be so, but my point is that she had something else to write. I've been racking my brain for something decent. If and when I do think of something half decent to write about, a few chapters in I find out it's a load of crap.'

'Have you ever thought of writing a prequel to *Killing Mr. Grey?*'

'A prequel?'

'Yeah!' the woman said, leaning forward excitedly, her eyes bright. 'Think about it. *Killing Mr. Grey* was about a love square among friends who had actually been enemies for a long time, right? Well, you can—'

'Eva! Your break's over,' the woman from behind the counter called.

'One minute,' Eva called, looking at her boss and then back at Billy. 'Think about it. You tell us what happens to lead up to the murder and we find out why it happened but not how, or really when. I think you should let us see when and how their love for each other turned to hate.'

'You know—' Billy began but was cut off when Eva's boss called her again. This time she held up her hand with her wristwatch on it.

'Sorry. I have to go because we are so busy that the

last customer who got served, I've been talking to for the last five minutes. You know, as soon as I finish my degree, I'm leaving this dump. I'm off to Hollywood.'

'You gonna be a screenwriter?'

Eva shook her head. 'Makeup artist, but if the makeup thing falls through, who knows. After all, I think I just came up with an idea for a bestseller.'

'I owe you,' he said, smiling.

'I'll take twenty percent.'

'I was thinking more along the lines of a dedication.'

'That too. Unlike most, I don't just buy my cake and let it sit there.'

'You know, I've never understood that phrase.'

'Me neither. I don't understand most of them. But listen, it was nice talking to you. I hope I've given you something to write about,' Eva said, smiling at him.

'More than enough. I'm sure you'll see your name in print pretty soon.' He said, watching as Eva gathered up her cup, saucer, and book.

'And a check in the mail,' she said, winking at him.

She turned and Billy watched her walk away, observing her slim but shapely hips sway from side to side. He sat there dumbfounded that in five minutes, he just had a better conversation with her than he'd had in six months of dating Natasha. Billy tore the plastic film from his notebook and began making notes.

Billy's cup of hot chocolate sat untouched as it went from hot to warm to undrinkable. He worked his pen across and down the page, ideas flowing like a tap that couldn't be turned off. He stayed hunched over his notebook, filling page after page. He didn't notice Eva smiling every time she glanced in his direction while she delivered food or wiped a table. Billy filled five pages of notes before he was satisfied that he had written enough. He closed his notebook, put the cap back on the pen, and stood up. Picking up his cup, Billy made his way over to the counter where the owner stood serving a customer. Eva was wiping down the top of the glass display counter.

'Thank you,' Billy said, holding out the cup. Eva took it from him with a smile, which faded as she saw the contents had not been touched.

'Was there something wrong with it?' she asked as Billy turned to walk away.

Billy turned back to face her and shrugged his shoulders. 'I wouldn't know. Other than it's way too cold to drink,' he said with a smile.

'One second,' Eva said, holding up one finger, indicating for him to wait, and she turned and quickly busied herself with making him a fresh one.

'You don't have to do that…Well, I suppose it was your fault,' Billy said jokingly, as Eva poured hot water into the paper cup and mixed it up with a wooden stirrer. She put a plastic lid on it and turned back to face him, holding it out for him to take.

'I would pay,' Billy said as he caught the grim look on the face of Eva's boss. 'It's just that I don't have any cash on me.'

'It's alright, I don't want my customers leaving unsatisfied,' she said with that weak smile of hers.

'Thanks, Eva,' Billy said, raising the cup almost as in a toast. 'I'm glad the other café was full.'

'Me too,' Eva replied, smiling.

There was a long silence before Billy realised he was standing there a bit too long.

'Bye,' he said, feeling a bit awkward as he turned and walked out of the café.

*

Who needs Facebook, Twitter, or even Sasha Grey when you had a notebook, a pen, and inspiration? Although the morning was a shitty one, the day had turned out to be his best day in a long while.

Billy decided to celebrate with a movie. What better way to celebrate than with the King of the Blockbusters, Mr Spielberg? Billy got a big bag of sweet and salty popcorn from the cupboard, poured himself a glass of Coke, and grabbed the half-empty bag of M&Ms. Billy spent the next twenty-five minutes staring at his Spielberg collection, trying to decide which he was more in the mood to watch. After going back and forth between *Jaws* and *War of the Worlds*, Billy pulled *War of the Worlds* from its place. After a long day of writing, Billy could do with something not so taxing on the brain and, although not better than *Jaws*, still a fun movie. Billy popped the disc into the Blu-ray player, grabbed the popcorn, and made himself comfortable on the sofa.

As a leaf with a drop of water on it filled the screen,

and Morgan Freeman started narrating, Billy stuffed a handful of popcorn into his mouth. Without taking his eyes from the screen, Billy reached down and found the Coke, picked up the glass, and took a gulp. He smiled with contentment, thinking to himself, '*Who indeed needed a PC and all that stuff that comes with it when you have the magic of Spielberg, the soothing voice of Morgan Freeman, and a thirty-two-inch flat screen? Yes, all was right with the world, thanks to my brother from another mother. And a new favourite girl, Eva. Not only pretty but pretty damn great in every*—'

Suddenly Billy's thought was broken as he realised that what he thought was a dissolve was too long to be a dissolve. Morgan Freeman was still narrating, and the screen was still blank.

'You've got to be shitting me!' Billy mumbled in frustration. Removing the popcorn from his lap, he pressed the on/off button on the remote control and the room went silent. He pushed it again and sighed with relief when the television came back on. Not only could he hear the narration, but he could see the picture to go with it. Billy picked up his popcorn again and settled back on the sofa as the film started.

Twenty minutes later, Billy was shovelling popcorn into his mouth and pouring Coke down his throat while Ray Ferrier ran down the street with the rest of the neighbourhood, trying to avoid the alien's death rays. Suddenly the living room went dark.

'You have to be shitting me!' Billy jumped up in frustration, causing popcorn to fly around the room.

He grabbed the remote from the arm of the sofa and pressed the on/off button again. This time there was still only audio and no visual. Billy repeated the process of pressing the on/off button, only to achieve the same result of sound but no picture.

'No way, dude!' Huy said, laughing on the other end of the phone as Billy finished telling him what had just happened. 'I don't mean to laugh, bro. I know it's not funny. Well, it is, but you get what I mean?'

'Yeah, I do,' Billy said drily.

'Also, just to let you know, these things happen in threes.'

'I fucking hope not,' Billy said worriedly. 'What's next, the fridge-freezer? I can't afford anything else to be breaking up on me.'

'I'm just saying that's what people say; bad luck always happens in bouts of three…Are you sure the TV is broken? Sometimes you just need to turn it off and on again at the mains,' Huy said to reassure him.

'Yes, I tried all of that before calling you,' Billy said, sighing with frustration.

'It seems like it's not your day today. First, the computer and now the television. It's not your day at all,' Huy said sympathetically.

'I'd say that too if I hadn't taken your advice and rediscovered the notebook and pen.

'And by doing that you came upon what?' Huy asked, after a long pause.

'A really cool girl.'

'Really,' Huy replied with intrigue.

'Yeah, after buying my notebook, I was gonna go into the posh café. You know that one with the exposed wooden flooring, the high stools, and all the fresh expensive shit…'

'You mean the one with the armchairs so comfortable that you fell asleep in one while I was talking to you?'

'Oh yeah, sorry about that,' Billy said, smiling.

'So she works there, does she?'

'Well, no. You see, it started raining, and as that one was full, I decided to go into that builders'-type one. You know, the one a few doors down where the owner has that look of permanent regret for having bought the place?'

'I may have passed. Can't say I've ever been in there.'

'I'm glad I have been! There's a girl who works there and Lord God…'

'The right amount of T&A, I take it?'

'Well to be honest, bro, I wasn't thinking of that. She was reading *The Postman Always Rings Twice.* That's what caught my attention first. But when she took her nose out of the book! I'm telling you, she had the face of an angel.'

'Correct me if I'm wrong, but didn't you say the same thing about Natasha? And look where that left you. Not being able to leave the house for six months and whining like a little bitch.'

'Well, I wouldn't put it quite like that,' Billy said, somewhat on the defensive side.

'Well, I call it as I see it, and that's what I saw. But to be honest, Billy, I may go on about tits and arse and everything in between, but when it comes down to it, those things don't really mean much if you don't get her and she doesn't get you.

Take Katie, for example. We fight like cats and dogs ten percent of the time, but the other ninety is me getting her, and her getting me. Not to mention that every time I see her is like the first time. For a moment, long or short, nothing else matters.'

'Huy, I didn't say I was in love with the girl. I just said there was an instant liking. Well, for me at least. But that's not all. She cured my writer's block and gave me an idea for my second book, bro.'

'Great. Let me know what she's like after the date.'

'What date?'

'You mean to tell me a beautiful girl talks to you, long enough to give you an idea for a novel and cures your writer's block and you don't ask her out? You know, Billy, I love you sometimes even more than my blood brother, but you know, like my real brother you can be such a prick. Take yourself down there right now and ask her out to dinner, a movie, or whatever. Telling me this girl has the face of an angel and enough sense upstairs to cure your block and you don't ask her out,' Huy said quietly, more to himself than to Billy.

'I can't. It's closed.'

'Well, make sure you're the first customer she serves in the morning. I'm off! And make sure you take care of all the other shit in your house. Something else is going to break. I just can't say what.'

'Okay, night Huy, and thanks for listening.'

'No worries. I'll be round on the weekend to look at the computer.'

'Thanks.'

'Night.'

*

Billy raised his hand and began to bring it down fast in a slapping motion towards his alarm clock and suddenly pulled his arm back towards his chest, sat up, and pressed the snooze button with his index finger. He lay back down, pleased that he had just saved his alarm clock. Sleeping was his third most favourite thing in the world, after writing, and reading. He'd sleep through anything, and that alarm clock had saved him from being late many times. But he didn't need it this morning.

With the ideas for his new book still floating around in his head, the worry about what was going to break on him next, and what he was going to say to Eva, Billy had been awake for the last half hour, staring up at the ceiling. Billy pushed the covers off and headed for the bathroom.

Twenty minutes later, Billy was showered and dressed. As he made himself breakfast, he went around the kitchen handling everything with care; opening the fridge door slowly when taking out the bread, milk, and margarine and closing it even more slowly. He filled the kettle with water and gently pressed the boil button and did the same with the lever as he put the bread in the toaster.

As he sat down at the table, he realised he could have just bought breakfast at the café. But if Eva rejected his offer of a date, that would be a bit awkward. So this was a much better plan. Also, who cared if a cup or saucer broke? For a moment, Billy thought of taking a cup or saucer from the drainer and dropping it on the floor in hopes that would be an end to his worries. But the three breakages have to be accidental, so breaking a cup or saucer would be a waste of time and money. The toast popped up from the toaster and Billy slowly got up and made his way over to the counter. He took a cup and saucer from the drainer, careful not to break anything, as the kettle came to a boil.

*

Having gone over what he was going to say a few times while walking to the café, Billy felt confident what he'd say was good enough. However, as he looked through the glass of the blue door, he saw a man standing in front of Eva and five or six customers seated at the tables.

'Shit,' he mumbled through gritted teeth, 'the morning rush.' He quickly pushed that thought away and entered the café confidently, his shoulders pulled back, and his head held high.

As he walked closer to the counter where the man was standing, his smile faded as he caught sight of the look on Eva's face. If looks could kill, the man would be dead. He was surprised that the man wasn't already sprawled out on the floor, ready to be taken away in a body bag. However, as he stood behind the customer, Billy began to understand why Eva wore the look of death.

'Well yeah, maybe I will have a jam sandwich instead of toast, but can you butter it first? Wait a minute, do you have peanut butter? You know, as the Americans do. I always thought it was a bit weird, but maybe I'll give it a try. Peanut butter and jam, or shall I use the term jelly, sandwich. And hold the cream with the coffee. I'll take it black. If I'm gonna do it like the Yanks, I'm gonna go all the way. In fact, maybe I should get a bagel instead. Yeah, yeah, make it a bagel and—'

'What!' Eva said fiercely. And suddenly the café went silent. The man she was serving went red in the face.

'Just a peanut butter and jam bagel, with a black coffee,' he said quietly, embarrassed as he looked slyly around at Billy and then back to Eva.

'Okay, so just to make sure. You want peanut butter and jam on a bagel, not a sandwich, with a black coffee. No milk, as we say in England.'

The man nodded in response and straightened his tie. 'I'll have it to take away, if you don't mind.'

'No problem. Take a seat, and I'll bring it to you.'

'Thanks,' the man said and walked away from the counter. Eva sighed as she watched him walk away.

As she noticed Billy standing there, the hardness in her eyes softened as a smile appeared.

'Sorry about that,' she said.

'Don't be. Personally, if I was you, I would have gone American too, turned into Muhammad Ali and punched him one.'

'I know, right?' she replied with a little laugh. 'For a moment, I had to restrain myself from turning into a murderer and doing him in with the butter knife. It may not be sharp, but I'm sure I could have made it work.'

'I'm glad you didn't. Doing life over some indecisive twit really isn't worth it.'

'I know. So, what can I get you?'

'A date. I was wondering if I could take you out for dinner this evening. You know, as payment for curing my writer's block.'

'No.'

'No?' Billy repeated in disbelief, his mouth gaping open and closed like a fish out of water.

'Did I stutter?'

'Do you mind me asking why?'

'You don't take someone out on a date just because they solved a problem for you. You go out with someone because you like them, and they like you, and you want to get to know them properly.'

'That's what I meant,' Billy said quickly. 'And also because she's got the face of an angel, except when she's thinking of doing someone in with a butter knife,' he said, smiling.

'That's better,' she replied with a little laugh.

'Lady, are you gonna serve me or stand there all day yapping?' a man standing behind Billy asked.

'One moment, mate. This is pretty important,' Billy said, looking at the man. Then he turned back to face Eva.

'So, is that a yes?'

'Sure.'

'Okay, meet me at seven outside the Crown and Castle pub in Dalston.'

'I'll be there,' Eva said, smiling.

'Okay, it's a date, and don't be late,' Billy said and began to make his way out of the café.

'Hey,' Eva called after him. 'How is my twenty percent coming along?'

'I'll let you know tonight, Angel Face,' Billy said coolly without looking back and exited the café.

*

Why is it that whenever you have all the time in the world and no particular place to be, bus drivers drive like their wives have been starving them of sex for the longest time? However, that morning before they left for work, their wives told them that the ban had been lifted and that if they made it home early, they could do whatever they wanted with them. In doing so, the person driving the bus leaves you clinging on to the bar in front of you and fearing for your life and praying silently. But when you've got somewhere to go, they drive like they have all day.

Billy sat upstairs at the front of the bus, silently cursing to himself as the traffic light went from green to amber to red, and the bus went from a slow crawl to a full stop.

He wasn't late yet, but he knew he wouldn't be there right on the dot. What if she was one of those people who hated waiting? If he had learned one thing for sure about Eva, it was that she hated being messed about. But he also knew that she was a cool girl, easy to talk to and funny, even if she was a bit scary. But it was just the right amount of scary, so you knew she meant business. He wanted to make a good impression, but this damn driver was going way too slow.

Finally, the traffic light turned green.

As the bus began to move, Billy got up and made his way down the stairs to the lower deck and pressed the bell.

As the bus stopped and the doors hissed open, Billy stepped into the rainy street. He looked at his wristwatch. It was two minutes past seven. He quickly pulled the hood of his coat over his head and hurried down the street as the rain poured down on him. He began weaving in and out of the pedestrians who were moving just as fast as he was to get out of the rain.

Taking a left, he finally got to the main road.

As he looked across the street, he saw Eva standing there waiting with an umbrella up, protecting herself from the rain. As he caught her eye, Billy began crossing the road. When she waved to him and smiled, for a moment nothing else mattered. Not the girl who dumped him without reason six months ago, or the book he had begun to write. He didn't worry about the TV that he couldn't watch anymore or the computer that would not turn on. Huy was right. Seeing someone as beautiful as the woman who stood across the road waiting for him made it seem like nothing else in the world mattered. Not even the car that crashed into him, sending him up into the air and back down to the ground, leaving him lifeless, broken.

Swing Little Girl

The sky was blue, and the clouds were puffy cotton balls of white. The sun was shining brightly. It was a good day for a visit to the park. It was a perfect day to swing, Amanda thought, as she made her way into the playground and looked up at the sky.

For most children, the playground, with its red slide, colourful roundabout, and its double swing frame, was just a place where kids came to cut loose for an hour or so after school or on the weekends. But for Amanda, it was once more than that; it was her special place where she came to escape the world.

Four years ago, for five straight weeks, there almost wasn't a day that went by that she wasn't here. And she wouldn't just spend an hour or two here either. She and Charles spent most of the day taking turns sliding down the slide, sometimes going down it together. Or they would go round and round on the roundabout, most of the time lying down on the yellow base and looking up at the sky while spinning. Other times they would be doing the thing she loved the most, swinging on the swing set. Sometimes swinging in time with each other, and other times racing one another or pushing each other. All the while, they talked about their hopes and dreams of the future and what they were going to do and be when they grew up. But most of the time they just sat on the swing and Charles listened to her as she read to him.

For the past four years, Amanda only came to the park once a year. It was still her special place, but it was no longer the happiest place on earth as it had once been. For the past four years, Amanda would only come to the park and head straight for 'her' swing, where she'd sit for hours in silence. Today, however, Amanda would try and make it like it was when she was a nine-year-old: the happiest place on earth, and for her and Charles, it was their Disneyland. So as Amanda entered the park, instead of going straight for 'her' swing, she walked over to the slide.

Amanda took hold of the ladder to climb the steps. She had to steady herself as the rickety ladder wobbled slightly. Amanda carefully climbed to the top, which seemed to take her far less time than it used to. She sat down, placing her hands on the warm metal sides. She looked down at the friendship bracelets she wore on her right wrist and closed her eyes and then pushed off and slid downwards, her long, blond hair covering her face as she went.

When Amanda reached the bottom, she stood up and combed her hair back from her face with her fingers as she made her way over to the roundabout. As she took hold of the red metal bar, she pushed once, and the roundabout turned slowly and then came to a stop. Amanda pushed it again and watched as the round metal object with its four yellow divided sections came to a halt once more. Amanda grabbed hold of the red bar and began to run with it. She ran as fast as she could until she could barely keep up with it and then jumped onto the yellow platform. Her hair flew up, and her pink cardigan puffed out as the roundabout began taking her around and around. Amanda grabbed onto the other bar, then pulled herself downwards into a sitting position, carefully placing her legs through the different dividing sections. She lay back, looking up at the bright blue sky and the puffy white clouds. Suddenly she was no longer thirteen anymore and as the roundabout turned around and around, the years rolled back too. Amanda let out a heartfelt giggle and wondered to herself what Charles would have thought if he was with her. 'Those clouds look so bouncy I'd like to jump on them.' Amanda found herself wondering if you really could bounce on puffy white clouds and if they were as soft as people often said they looked.

As the roundabout came to a stop, Amanda got to her feet. When she stepped down off the roundabout, she had to steady herself, as her head was still spinning and her legs wobbled.

When she felt her legs stabilise, she began slowly walking over to the swing set. On the way, she enjoyed wondering if you could bounce on clouds, even if it was childish. But that's what she did with Charles. He was always thinking of silly things like that, but whenever he said something, he always made her smile or laugh. He didn't speak much, but when he did, he made it count.

Amanda sat down on the swing on the left of the swing set, as she had done nearly every day during the five weeks they had spent together, and began to rock backwards and forwards slightly. As she did, she took hold of the empty swing next to her and started pushing it.

Suddenly she stopped and looked around, just in case anyone was watching. No one was watching. Two thoughts occurred to her; first, whenever she and Charles were in the park, it was always empty, no matter how hot it was, except that one time. It was just like he said to her, 'This will be our special place, the happiest place on earth, just like Disneyland.' It was whenever they were here together.

Second, she told herself not to care. Even if a hundred people were watching, big or small, she would do it anyway; for Charles, she would do anything. He'd like what she was doing, and that was all that mattered. He was her best friend! Even from their first meeting, deep down, she knew he was a good one. She just would not allow herself to believe it at first. However, as soon as she did, there wasn't a day they weren't together. He was always there for her. He saved her every day from the first day they met, especially on the first day.

*

Four years earlier, nine-year-old Amanda Curtis tore open the front door of her two-story detached house and ran down the path as she escaped the clutches of her father.

If someone had come along and told her that summer was going to be the best summer ever, she would have given them the middle finger. And if that same person had told her she was going to find her best friend, the best friend she'd ever have, she would have either given them a fist to their mouth or some saliva to their face. There was no summer! As far as Amanda was concerned, summer meant bright blue skies (even in England) filled with days out in the sun and lots of fun. It was never sunny or bright, in Amanda's opinion, even when it was very bright and sunny. And she certainly didn't have any friends. Not real-life friends anyway. Her friends were Dickens, Austen, Dahl, and many other people whom she only knew from the pages of her books. She had no real friends. She didn't even have a mother.

To Amanda, a mother was as real as Santa Claus or the Easter Bunny. When she was at school and saw other mothers dropping their children off or picking them up, they didn't seem real. The only person whom Amanda had was her father. And she didn't want him, ever! Today she was going to finally make that clear.

'You get back here right now!' her father raged, as he lunged forward out of the house and onto the path.

As Amanda reached the far end of the path, she spun around, her cheeks hot pink, her blue eyes full of rage as tears welled up in them.

'No! I never want to be near you again, do you hear me? Never again!' Amanda screamed back at him. She looked to her right and eyed the red sports convertible, took the few steps towards it, and began kicking.

'Never! Ever! Again!' she yelled, kicking the side of the car.

'Why you little fucking shit!' her father hissed at her through gritted teeth and began to run down the path after her. Seeing him coming, Amanda turned and ran down the road, her father's legs slowing as she did so.

When Amanda was well out of range, her father scanned the street carefully, checking to see if any onlookers had witnessed the commotion. No one was watching. Amanda's father sucked in a deep breath and then let it out. He took a few steps over to his beloved convertible. He inspected the wheel and the area above it where Amanda had kicked at it. Just a few scuff marks and a small footprint from her Nike trainers, he thought, rubbing at the footprint and seeing it come off on his hand.

Amanda's father sighed heavily and straightened up. He turned and began to walk back up the path. As he got halfway up the path, a light wind began to blow. Feeling a chill, he looked around and quickly pulled his trouser zipper up and continued walking up the path towards the house. He stepped inside and closed the door with a snap.

Amanda ran across the road. As she got to the other side, she turned to see if her father was coming up behind her. When she saw he was nowhere in sight, she paused to catch her breath for a few moments. She turned down a side road, making her way up a small alleyway. Coming out of the alley, she came onto a small, caged playground.

She made her way over to the entrance and walked through it, passing the slide and the roundabout. She didn't even notice the little black boy who was lying down on the yellow platform, looking up at the sky as the roundabout slowly turned around. Amanda stopped as she approached the red-framed swing set and sat down on the yellow plastic seat.

She sat there rocking back and forth ever so slightly, thinking how rubbish her life was and wondering if it was this way for other children. *'If my mother was alive, would this be happening?'* Amanda wondered. Even though this thought often came to her, she always came to the same conclusion: her mother didn't even stick around for her arrival. As soon as Amanda appeared, her mother went. She was as dead as a doornail before Amanda stopped crying, still in the arms of the nurse.

Over the years, whenever Amanda's father mentioned her mother, he'd always say, 'Be grateful, little girl. She died so you could live.' And Amanda went with it for a while. But as Amanda got older and that phrase floated out of his mouth, Amanda thought the real reason that her mother died was to escape him.

Amanda often found herself wishing that she would have died, too. But death seemed too painful, and she didn't need any more of that.

Besides, death meant never reading *Oliver Twist* or *Pride and Prejudice* or *Matilda* again and never being able to be with the only things that made her comfortable. Worse than death, she didn't know if you could read in heaven. If death came, it came. She wouldn't do it herself, but she didn't shun the idea either.

Amanda walked back with the swing underneath her, setting it in motion. She began pumping her legs back and forth as she got the swing moving. Amanda stood up and started working the swing hard and fast, back and forth, as tears began to roll down her cheeks. She worked the swing harder, going faster and faster and higher and higher. Suddenly Amanda felt herself losing her balance. She grabbed for the linked chains and caught hold of one, but she felt her foot slipping from the seat. Amanda began to fall when suddenly she felt something stabilise the swing and herself.

As the swing came to a stop, Amanda turned to see a small black boy holding the swing in place for her.

'You know, you should be more careful. You could really hurt yourself doing that. This is concrete,' the little boy said matter of factly, as Amanda sat on the swing. But when the boy saw that Amanda had been crying, his tone changed. 'What's wrong?' he asked softly, his voice full of concern.

'Nothing!' Amanda snapped, wiping her tears.

'It's okay. You can tell me. We could be friends,' the boy said, putting his arm around Amanda's shoulder. Amanda flinched at his touch and jumped off the swing.

'Don't touch me! I don't like it.'

'W-what, what did I do?' the boy asked, confused at her reaction.

Amanda walked over to the chipped red swing frame and slid down onto the ground into a sitting position. As she leaned against the frame, she covered her face with her hands and began to cry. The boy saw her beginning to shake and walked over to her.

'Would you like me to take you home?' the boy asked, crouching down so he was level with Amanda.

'No!' Amanda shouted, looking up at him as she wiped at her tears.

'I could help you; I'm a helpful boy. We could be friends.'

'I don't need your help, and I don't want to be your friend,' Amanda said, getting to her feet and walking over to the empty swing seat. Amanda sat down, rocking back and forth on her heels, staring at the ground, tears still lingering in her eyes.

'Are you sure you don't want me to take you home? I can do it, you know. I've been crossing roads all by myself for two years now.'

Amanda shook her head softly. 'I'm not going home. I'll stay right here.'

'Can I stay with you?'

'Do as you please, I don't own the park,' she said, still staring at the ground.

The little boy stood watching Amanda for a long while.

'You gonna stand there staring at me all day?' she asked, finally looking at him.

The boy shrugged and walked over to the empty swing, climbed up on it, and sat down.

'What's your name?' the boy asked, not knowing what else to say.

'Amanda.'

'Well Amanda, I'm Charles; Charles Nicholas Carter, and it's very nice to meet you,' the little boy said, holding out his small hand for her to shake while giving her the brightest smile he could muster.

Amanda eyed the little boy's hand for a long moment, then took hold of it. 'I'm Amanda Alison Curtis.'

When she shook the little boy's hand, she really looked at him for the first time. He was a few inches smaller than Amanda. Where her feet were firmly on the ground, his toes just missed it. He had a little unkempt afro, and his blue jeans were well worn at the knees. He wore a jumper, which was ripped at the shoulder and badly frayed at the bottom. He was sporting a black and blue bruise around his right eye; eyes that, even without the injury, looked dull and tired. Looking at him, Amanda thought to herself that the name Oliver would have suited him better than Charles.

'You know your name is the same name as my favourite author.'

'What's his name?'

'Charles Dickens.'

'Who is he?'

'He's my favourite author.'

'What's that?'

'An author? Don't you know what an author is?'

Charles shook his head.

'It's someone who writes books,' Amanda said simply.

'Oh yeah,' he said quietly.

After that, the two children sat quietly for a long time.

Eventually, Charles dug his hand into his pocket and took out a package wrapped in tin foil and unwrapped it to revel two custard creams and held it out for her to take one. 'Would you like a biscuit?'

Amanda reached out to take one, then stopped.

'You only have two,' she said, letting her hand drop back into her lap.

'That's okay. You look like you need it more than me. I love custard creams; they are so yummy, and they make me happy,' Charles said, grinning happily.

Amanda smiled as he did, noticing that he was missing a tooth, and she took a custard cream from the tin foil package. 'Thank you,' Amanda said and held it in her hand for a long moment as she rocked back and forth.

'Aren't you going to eat it?' Charles asked, watching Amanda eagerly as though he had made the biscuit himself and was waiting to see what she thought of it.

'Let's eat it together,' Amanda replied.

'Yeah, that's a good idea,' Charles said, smiling as the two children began to eat their custard creams.

'Good, ain't it?' Charles said, his eyes full of delight.

'Yes, very,' Amanda agreed.

'What happened to your eye?' Amanda asked.

'Oh…my brother did it,' Charles replied, and the silence returned.

'Do you come here often?' Amanda said, feeling the need to break the silence.

'Yes, every time I don't have school. It's my special place. You know, if you want, it could be our special place. We could be friends; we could be a team. That's our roundabout, and that's our slide and these swings. That can be your swing and this mine,' Charles said earnestly.

'And what if someone else wants a go?' Amanda asked, playing along.

'We won't let them on; it's our place.'

'But what if someone comes when one of us is not here? What then?'

'I will keep it safe for you. Don't worry, this place is magic. Like Disneyland.'

'Have you ever been?' Amanda inquired.

'To Disneyland, no. But I see it on the TV, and it says it's full of magic and it's the happiest place on earth.' One day I'm gonna go. Or maybe if you want to be my friend, we can go together. We can meet all the gang, Mickey, and Goofy, and Donald, and we can go on all the rides and have lots of fun and eat lots of sweets, like ice cream and cakes and chocolate! It will be so much fun. That will have to be when I am older because then I'm going to have lots of money. Right now I don't have any so I can't go. But when

I'm older, I will. If you don't have money, I'll pay for you. I will, honest.'

Amanda nodded, smiling briefly and humouring him.

'But now we have to settle for this place. I don't mind, though,' he said, smiling back at her.

'I guess that would be fun,' she replied, and then stood up off the swing.

'I'm gonna go now, but it was nice talking to you.'

'Really?' Charles asked disappointedly.

'Yes.'

'Oh, okay,' Charles said softly. 'It was nice meeting you too, Amanda.'

Amanda lifted her arm and waved at him and then turned and started walking away.

'Amanda!' Charles called out, and she turned to face him.

'Yes?'

'Why do you have a fish on your bracelet?'

'It's not just a bracelet; it's a friendship bracelet.'

'Do you have lots of friends?' Charles asked with disappointment in his voice.

Amanda shook her head. 'It's called a friendship bracelet. I made it myself. The fish is my sign,' Amanda said, lifting up her sleeve and showing him the threaded pink and green friendship bracelet with a pink fish charm hanging from it.

'You made that?' Charles asked in awe.

'Yes. I really enjoy making these.'

'You must be very clever,' Charles said, impressed.

'Goodbye, Charles,' Amanda said and turned back towards the gate.

'Amanda?'

'Yes?' Amanda said, beginning to feel annoyed.

'I'll be seeing you.'

'Huh?' she replied in confusion.

'Tomorrow. Will you come tomorrow?' he asked with hope in his voice.

'Maybe,' she replied.

'Okay great, I'll be seeing you,' Charles said, grinning as he waved at her. Amanda waved back and then turned and walked out the park gate.

*

Charles didn't see Amanda the day after they met or even the day after that. Amanda didn't even give Charles another thought after she left the park that day. Why should she? Amanda didn't need another friend. She had all the 'friends' she wanted. If it wasn't for the 'friends' she went to buy the week after she had met Charles, Amanda probably wouldn't have given Charles another thought ever. However, after the bookshop, Amanda decided to stop by the corner shop and buy some chocolate. That required passing by the park.

As the park came into view, Amanda glanced in that direction. Her heart leapt into her throat, and she broke into a sprint. She saw a boy even taller than herself, putting Charles in a chokehold! Amanda ran into the park, and threw her book bag down on the ground. She ran to where Charles was held up against the red swing frame. She grabbed the back of the bully's t-shirt and yanked him away. The boy stumbled backwards, partly due to surprise and partly because of Amanda's strength.

'Leave him alone!' Amanda shouted angrily, stepping in front of Charles and blocking him from harm.

Charles's hand went to his throat, and he began rubbing it as he panted, struggling to recover his breath. The bully regained his footing and made a grab for Amanda, but she slapped his hand away and started pounding him with her fist in a frenzy. The bully curled up defensively as Amanda kept pounding him, not caring where her fists were landing, until the bully finally turned and ran from the park. Amanda walked away from the swing set, breathing hard, her cheeks pink.

'Amanda!' Charles called after her as she walked. Amanda turned around to see him.

'Where are you going?'

'To get my books,' she replied and then turned back in the direction of her book bag, where two of the three fat novels lay scattered on the ground. Charles walked quickly towards her.

'Thank you, Amanda,' he said, catching up with her. Amanda said nothing as she bent down and picked up a book. Charles reached down and picked up the other book and held it out for Amanda as she picked up the carrier bag. She took the book from Charles and stood there staring at him. He wore a black t-shirt with Mickey Mouse on it that was far too big for him and reached halfway down his red shorts.

'What happened?' she asked softly.

'He wanted to use the swing and I said he couldn't.'

'Why didn't you just let him use the swing, it would have saved you a lot of trouble?'

'Because it's your swing, remember? I was saving it for you,' Charles said, looking past Amanda towards the swing.

'You were saving the swing for me?' Amanda asked, surprised.

'I said I would, didn't I?' he said, sounding offended.

'All week?'

'All week,' replied Charles as he began walking over to the swing set. He stopped when he realised Amanda wasn't following him. He turned and beckoned her over with a small wave of the hand and Amanda finally began to walk towards him.

Charles pointed at the swing set, smiling as Amanda looked at it too.

Then she noticed a white piece of paper taped to the seat by two stickers of football players at both ends. Written in untidy scroll were the words, 'This swing is not in use. Manager of the Park.'

'Pretty good idea, huh! I got my mum to help me with the spelling,' Charles said, grinning. He was pretty pleased with himself, already forgetting that all but moments ago he was nearly choked to death because of it.

'Wanna race me?' Charles asked, smiling hopefully, as he looked up at her. Amanda tilted her head to the side, thoughtfully, and then nodded.

'Sure, why not.'

'Great!' Charles said as he climbed onto the swing. Amanda placed the book bag by the frame and walked back over to the swing. She stared down at the white piece of paper with its messy scroll for a long time before she sat on the swing.

'Are you ready?' Charles asked, smiling at her as she nodded. 'Okay on three! One, two, three,' Charles counted softly as they both began to swing. Pumping their legs as fast as they could, they both went higher and higher. Charles giggled a lot and Amanda began to laugh, too.

Charles won the race to the top, but as their swings slowed down, neither said anything. They just went back up again, swinging higher and laughing harder. They did it five more times before they had to stop and catch their breath. As they did, Charles's eyes fell on the book bag again.

'Those books sure are big; they must have lots and lots of pictures in them!' Charles said.

'They don't have any pictures in them. Well, one does. But the other two don't have any,' Amanda replied.

'No pictures?' Charles exclaimed in bewilderment. 'If they have no pictures in them, how are you meant to know what's going on?'

'You use your imagination. As you read, your imagination will show you everything,' Amanda said.

'I don't read so good,' Charles said, barely above a whisper.

'I love to read. For me, there is nothing better. You see, reading is like playing. When you play, you imagine, right? Well, that's just like books with no pictures. When you read books with no pictures, you imagine what you want to, not what the pictures tell you to.'

'Yeah but the pictures go with the words!'

'And so does your mind.' It went silent as Charles thought about what she was saying.

Amanda got off the swing and walked over to the bag of books by the swing frame. She picked it up and walked back over to her swing and sat down. 'Okay, Charles, where would you like to go?'

'Huh?' Charles asked.

'I'm gonna read to you.'

'Really?' Charles said happily.

'Yeah, sure. Why not?'

'Wow! No one has read to me since my dad left.'

'Your mum doesn't?'

'No, she has never read to me.'

'What did your dad read to you?'

'When I was very young, about four or so, we would read *The Tiger Who Came to Tea* and *Not Now, Bernard*. Picture books, see. But I'm not sure if that was real because when I asked my mum to read to me and…and she said no. I told her that I liked my father better because he would and then she told me to shut up and that I was talking nonsense.'

'Doesn't your father live with you anymore?' Amanda asked softly, seeing his eyes become glossy.

Charles shook his head and looked down at the ground.

'Was he a good man?'

'The best,' Charles said, swiping at a tear and then looking up at her. 'He would not only read to me, but we played games, watched movies, and we would eat popcorn. Then one day I woke up and he wasn't there anymore. So now it's just me and Mummy,' Charles said.

'And your brother,' Amanda added.

'My brother…Oh, yes me, Mummy, and my brother. Just us three. No father to play games or watch movies or read to me,' Charles said, allowing one tear to fall and then swiping at another.

'It's okay, Charles. I can read to you,' Amanda said softly. 'Where would you like to go first? We can go to Narnia, or we could go and see the Bennet's in Hertfordshire or we could go to Maycomb.'

'Can I see the covers?' Charles asked, and Amanda pulled the books from the bag and handed them to him. He could see the covers of *The Magician's Nephew*, *Pride and Prejudice*, and *To Kill a Mockingbird*. Charles chose *The Magician's Nephew*.

As Amanda began to read to him, Charles was no longer in the park but transported to Narnia with Digory, Polly, and the Wicked Witch, and the strange and magical creatures of Narnia. Amanda sat reading while Charles sat listening, not uttering a word.

Amanda stopped eventually, and they sat in silence as the sun began its descent.

'I best get going,' Charles finally said. 'It's getting dark. Would you like me to walk you home?' he asked.

'No, but maybe I should walk you home,' Amanda replied.

'It's okay. It's only down the path, around the corner past the shop, then up the road, down the road, and round another corner and then I'm home.'

'Only?' Amanda said, a small smile playing on her lips. 'Let me walk with you. I'll feel much better,' Amanda said.

'Okay, but I'm a big boy, you know. I can cross roads and everything.'

'I know. You told me that when we first met last week,' Amanda replied as the two set off from the park.

They walked down the path, around the corner, past the shop, then up the road, down the road, and round another corner to where Charles lived, not saying a single word. Even though they didn't say anything, they both enjoyed the walk as they thought over the day's events.

'That's my house,' Charles said as they came to a row of houses, all identical with small front gardens and brown wooden fences. Charles pointed to the house at the end of the street with the overgrown weeds and a broken cooker in the garden. Amanda walked Charles to his front gate. As Charles pushed the broken brown picket gate open, it scraped across the concrete path.

'Thanks for today, Amanda. Thanks for saving me from that boy.'

'It's okay. I'm glad I did, after that we had fun, didn't we?' she said.

'Lots,' he agreed. 'You know, one day I'm going to read just as good as you do. Because you took me there, it felt like I was really in Narnia.'

'And we aren't even finished yet,' she said, smiling.

'So, you will read to me again,' Charles said, his brown eyes dancing with happiness.

'Tomorrow.'

'Wow, wicked! So, I'll be seeing you.'

'I'll be seeing you,' Amanda replied, waving to him. She watched as Charles scraped the gate closed and turned to walk up to his front door. He turned to her once more, waved, and then gave her a thumbs up. She raised a hand to him and smiled. Charles grinned happily, baring his missing tooth, and then turned and put his key in the door. As Charles went in and closed the door, Amanda began walking down the street. She felt a strange something in her that she could not remember ever feeling…happiness.

*

The next day when Amanda got to the park, she saw Charles sitting on the roundabout as it turned around slowly. Seeing her, he took hold of the bar and stood up and waved, his face brightening considerably as she made her way towards the roundabout, books in hand.

'Hello, Amanda,' Charles said, smiling happily.

'Hello,' she said, smiling back. 'Are you ready to go back to Narnia?'

'Been waiting since last night.'

'Well, let's do this then,' Amanda said and headed for the swing set. Charles jumped off the slowly moving roundabout and followed her.

'Not that one. This is your swing, remember?' Charles exclaimed as he pointed to the swing that still had the sign taped to it with the football stickers.

'Oh, sorry,' Amanda said as she moved to the swing on the left side and sat on it.

'Hey, you know what? Maybe I can push you while you read to me?' Charles said.

'Are you sure you can manage?' Amanda asked.

'Yeah, I'm not that much younger than you,' Charles said, pausing thoughtfully. 'How old are you, anyway?'

'Nine. I was nine in March.'

'Oh really, I was eight in September, but that doesn't matter. I can still do it,' he said as he walked around to the back of the swing. 'Ready?' he asked.

Amanda opened the page to where they left off yesterday, and adjusted herself so she was sitting firmly on the swing, holding the chain with one hand and the book in the other.

'Ready,' she said, and although she had her doubts, she was pleasantly surprised when Charles easily pushed her. She began to read to him as the swing went back and forth, slowly but consistently. When Charles's arms became tired, Amanda would push him with one hand while reading from the book that she held in the other.

*

'So, shall we now go to Hertfordshire where Netherfield is about to be let?' Amanda asked as they returned from Narnia. She closed the book as she sat on the swing and turned to look at Charles, who was still pushing her. Charles nodded gleefully, so Amanda got off the swing and traded *The Magician's Nephew* for *Pride and Prejudice*.

'Oh, wait! We can take a break first!' Charles said, standing. From one pocket he pulled out two shiny packages of tin foil and handed one to her. From his other pocket, he pulled an old cola bottle filled with orange squash.

'I didn't have another bottle, but we can share this one if you like,' Charles said, looking at her regretfully.

'I'd like that,' Amanda said as she sat on her swing. She unwrapped the tinfoil package to reveal two custard creams. Charles took his seat on the swing and opened his tinfoil package and took a bite of his biscuit.

'You know, Amanda, I never thought being read to

could be so good,' he said, brushing the crumbs from his plain blue t-shirt.

'I know. It's great, right? I love it,' Amanda replied, also taking a bite of her biscuit. Charles folded the foil back over his biscuits and placed them on his lap and then opened the bottle of squash and took a sip. He gave the bottle to Amanda, who drank some and then handed the bottle back to him. Charles put the cap back on the bottle and made sure it was screwed on tightly. Taking hold of his foil package, he then jumped down off the swing and put the bottle back in his pocket and started inspecting his clothes.

'What are you doing, Charles?' Amanda asked, looking at him with suspicion.

'I can't get my clothes dirty. My mum gets mad at me, saying that she doesn't have enough money to keep washing them. That's why I like to keep them as clean as possible,' he said, brushing at his t-shirt and shorts.

'Oh,' Amanda said, feeling conscious, and checked her bright pink t-shirt with a unicorn on it. She brushed at the crumbs that had fallen onto it and then brushed off her jeans as well.

'Shall we begin? It looks much bigger than the Narnia one,' Charles said as he sat back down on the swing.

'It is,' Amanda said, standing up and moving over to the frame, picking up the paperback copy of *Pride and Prejudice*. She sat back down on the swing and opened the book halfway and showed Charles the size of the font.

'Wow, the writing is smaller too.'

'So, you ready?' Amanda asked, and Charles nodded happily. Amanda turned to the title page and cleared her throat.

'*Pride and Prejudice* by Jane Austen,' she read.

Amanda and Charles began their journey into Hertfordshire with the Bennet sisters and their mother's quest to marry them off to the wealthiest man as soon as possible.

Charles was right. *Pride and Prejudice* did take much longer for them to read than *The Magician's Nephew*, and Charles had lots of questions about the book. Amanda readily gave the best answers she could when he asked. Even though there were many questions, and sometimes they stopped reading altogether to race each other on the swings, ride the roundabout, or take turns on the slide, reading was their primary objective now.

Each day when Amanda got to the park, Charles was always there waiting for her, ready to listen. He often had a question about what they had read the day before that he spent most of the night thinking about up in his room.

They had been visiting Hertfordshire for five days and were halfway through the book. On day six, Amanda woke, got out of bed, and removed the chair from under the door handle. She ran to the bathroom, where she quickly took a shower and got ready for another day at the park. She put on her light pink jeans and her pastel green t-shirt, grabbed hold of *Pride and Prejudice*, and made her way downstairs to the front door.

'Shit!' she hissed as she saw the rain. It wasn't heavy rain, but it sure wasn't park weather.

Amanda slammed the door shut and went back upstairs to her room, walked over to her bed, and plunked down on it. She looked down at the book and then opened it. A moment later, she snapped it closed again. She couldn't read it now, not without Charles. That would ruin it. She sighed heavily and lay on her bed.

She needed to get out. After what seemed like an eternity of staring up at the ceiling, Amanda sat upright. She walked over to her chest of draws, opened the second drawer and took out a black hoodie, and then grabbed her green North Face rain jacket and put it on.

Opening the front door, she pulled her hood up over her head, stepped out of the house, and closed the front door. Amanda walked down the alley and came out by the park. As she neared the park, she looked at it in annoyance, thinking she and Charles wouldn't be reading today. As she walked by the park, her eyes fell on a person sitting under the slide. Amanda crossed the road to take a closer look. As she got closer, she saw that it was Charles sitting under the slide frame, dressed in black jeans and a thin raincoat.

Amanda walked over to the slide and bent down. 'Hello, Charles, what are you doing here? You'll catch your death.'

'Hello, Amanda. I didn't know you were going to come here today,' he said softly.

'Of course not! It's raining! What are you doing here? You'll catch a cold if you are not careful.'

'It's okay; I always come here when it's raining.'

'But why? Do you like the rain?' Amanda asked, confused.

'No.'

'Then why are you out sitting in it?'

'Because it's quiet; there are fewer people about when it's raining. No one is shouting at you or moaning at you, and I like the sound as the rain hits things. Come.' Charles patted the ground for Amanda to come under the silver base and sit next to him.

'You're reading,' Amanda said happily, as she sat next to him. She noticed that Charles was holding a copy of *Not Now Bernard*.

'It's not the same anymore,' Charles said grumpily.

'You mean without your dad here to read it?'

'No, I mean it doesn't have enough words in it for me to picture it as good as I did when you were reading *Narnia*, or *Pride and Prejudice*. It's for babies,' Charles said in a huff. 'Can we read *Pride and Prejudice*? We can go to your house and…'

'No!' Amanda snapped, her nostrils flaring, her cheeks growing red.

'But—' Charles murmured.

'I don't care,' Amanda said, panic rising in her voice. 'If you ever come to my house, I swear to you I'll never read to you again. Ever!' she said, her eyes wide and fearful.

'Okay,' Charles murmured again.

'Promise me.'

'I promise,' Charles said, worriedly.

'Do as I do,' Amanda said, and she held out her hand and spat in her palm and Charles did the same.

'Now we shake,' she said, and the two children shook hands, their spit making a squishy sound as their hands joined, cementing their promise. 'Our hands are bricks and our spit cement binding our promise together forever, which means it can never be broken,' she said, holding Charles's hand firmly.

'Okay, I will never break it. I won't ever come to your house.' Seeing the earnest look on Charles's face, Amanda began to relax, and her cheeks began to return to their normal colour. She removed her hand from his, and the two children just sat in silence as the rain came down.

'Hey, Charles,' Amanda said, after they had been sitting in silence for ten minutes or so. When Charles didn't answer, she turned to see him with his eyes closed. 'Charles,' she called again, placing a hand on his shoulder.

Charles raised a small hand. 'It's raining, and I'm walking to Netherfield with Elizabeth across muddy fields. I'll be back soon,' he said, calmly placing his hand in his lap. Amanda fell silent again, grinning as she did so.

Ten minutes later, she called him again.

'Charles,' she said softly, and this time Charles opened his eyes and turned to face her.

'Would you like to go back to Hertfordshire today?' she asked.

'But you said we can't go to your house to get the book.'

'We don't have to,' Amanda said, grinning. 'So do you wanna?'

'Of course,' Charles said, nodding enthusiastically.

'Then come on then, and this time I will show you my favourite place ever.'

'Okay, great! Is it far?'

'Not really, it's a little walk. We can have a walking adventure.'

'Okay,' Charles said, quickly getting up. 'So, what are we waiting for?' he said when he saw Amanda still sitting on the ground looking up at him. 'Let's go, the quicker we get there, the more we'll get to read.'

'I've been waiting for ten minutes, Charles. It's what I wanted to tell you when I called you the first time.'

'Sorry,' Charles said, holding out his hand for Amanda to take. Charles helped her to her feet, and the two children left the park.

*

They walked in silence, Amanda only speaking to tell Charles where to turn. Twenty minutes later, they were outside Nicola's Books. The wooden shopfront was painted red and had two large bay windows on either side of the door, displaying the latest publications and best sellers.

'Books!' Charles said, happily looking at Amanda.

'Lots of them,' she said, grinning back at him. Amanda walked forward and pulled the door open, holding it for Charles to walk through. A bell chimed, welcoming them.

'Thank you,' Charles said, as he passed Amanda and entered the shop. Amanda walked in after him and closed the door behind her.

Charles looked around the single-story building in fascination. He had passed by book shops, but never really felt the urge to enter one. After all, Charles didn't read and had no one to read to him before. Now he stood inside the shop, taking in the floor-to-ceiling shelves filled with books and the display tables placed around the shop floor.

There was even a coffee shop at the back of the store. Charles could hear spoons being tapped against cups and cups hitting saucers and the hissings of the coffee machines. He could see people sitting at tables, enjoying their favourite drink or cake or even both while reading a book or a newspaper. Charles's mind began to realise what he had been missing; could this be better than the park?

'Hey, Charles!' Amanda called, bringing Charles back to the moment; she was now in front of him. 'Come on, let's go get the book.'

'Oh yeah, sure,' he replied, and the two children weaved their way through the customers who were browsing the shelves and tables. They made their way over to the payment counter and joined the queue of people who were waiting to pay for their goods.

'Hello, Miss Carnegie!' Amanda said, smiling brightly up at Nicola Carnegie, a thin black lady with a friendly face and warm hazel eyes. Miss Carnegie wore a red turtle-neck jumper and had thick, brown, horn-rimmed glasses that hung on a gold chain from her neck and rested just below her breast. She looked at Amanda and Charles, her hazel eyes twinkling as the two children stepped up to the counter.

'Hello, Amanda, how are you today and who is your friend?'

'I'm okay, Miss Carnegie. This is Charles.'

'Hello, Charles,' Miss Carnegie said, turning to face him. Charles stuck out his hand for her to shake.

'Charles Carter, ma'am.'

'Miss Carnegie, if you will, Charles. Never anything else,' she said, warmly, and Charles nodded.

'What can I do for you two today?' she said, turning to the both of them.

'Is it okay if we sit in here and read today? Charles and me? We have been reading *Pride and Prejudice* in the park, but it's raining, and I didn't bring my copy.'

'You go right ahead. Are you enjoying it?'

'Oh, it's the best! I can't wait to get to the end and see what happens to Elizabeth and Mr. Darcy. Have you read it?' Charles asked eagerly.

'Charles, if I hadn't, I wouldn't have the right to be standing where I am now. It's one of my favourites,' she said, with a big grin on her face.

'Mine, too,' Charles replied, grinning back at her.

'Okay, Miss Carnegie, we'll go sit in the café. Speak to you later.'

'Enjoy, and it was nice to meet you, Charles.'

'You too, Miss Carnegie,' Charles said, waving to her.

'Oh, and Amanda…'

'Yes?'

'It's not 'Charles and me,' but Charles and I. I thought you knew better than that?'

'I'm sorry. It won't happen again.'

'It's okay. You both enjoy the book,' Miss Carnegie said, waving back at them. As Charles and Amanda walked away, Miss Carnegie beckoned to the next customer in line.

'Amanda, does that lady own the shop?' Charles asked as they walked towards the fiction section.

'Yes,' Amanda replied.

'So why does she have Nicola on the front of the shop if her name is Miss Carnegie?'

'Because her name is Nicola Carnegie. This is how she explained it to me…Would you call your mother by her given name?' Amanda asked.

'No,' Charles replied.

'Why not?'

'I'm not allowed, out of respect,' he said.

'Correct. Miss Carnegie thinks that children don't have enough respect anymore. She hates hearing children saying 'what' when they should be saying 'yes.' 'What's up' instead of 'hello' and it's the same for names. 'Miss Carnegie' is for children to use, just like when you're at school. It's more respectful. When you give respect, you get it. In most cases…That is how she explained it to me,' Amanda said as they reached the A's in the fiction section.

'Excuse me, sir,' Amanda said to the man who stood next to them, browsing the shelves as he held a briefcase in one hand and a wet umbrella in the other.

'Hello.'

'Hi! Please, could you pass me the hardcover copy of *Pride and Prejudice*?' Amanda asked, smiling.

'Sure,' the man said. He put his briefcase down and reached for the book, pulled it from the shelf, and handed it to her.

'Thank you, sir. Have a nice day,' Amanda said, smiling at him.

'You're welcome,' the man said and smiled back at her.

'Thank you, sir,' Charles said.

'You're welcome, too,' the man said and smiled at Charles.

Amanda took a few steps away from the shelf then stopped, opened the book, stuck her nose into it, and inhaled.

'I love the smell of new books,' she said, bringing her head up again.

'Let me,' Charles said, and she allowed him to smell the book.

'Yes, it does smell nice. Tell me, Amanda, what made you first start reading?'

'My teacher, Mrs Chivers. She was the best. When she found out I could read well, she'd bring me different books to read than the rest of the class.

I'd read everything she gave me as fast as I could. Then I'd ask my father for money to buy them, and I'd stay up late at night rereading them. I'm telling you, Charles, books are the things that keep me going. I don't know where I'd be without them.'

'Huh,' Charles said, confused.

'I mean that I could spend all day reading them.'

'Oh, cool!' Charles said happily, 'Does that mean I keep you going, too? You've been spending a lot of time reading with me.'

'I guess,' Amanda said, thinking about the sinking feeling she had this morning when she opened the front door and saw the rain coming down. She thought that she wouldn't be seeing Charles that day.

'Does this mean we are friends? Because I think we could be really good friends,' Charles said, with hope in his voice.

'I think so, too,' she replied.

'So we are?' Charles said, his normally dull brown eyes beginning to brighten.

'Yes,' Amanda said, smiling at him. 'We are friends.'

'Wicked!' Charles exclaimed with glee. 'Let's get on with the book! The quicker we read this, the quicker we can move on to the next.'

'Okay.'

The children walked towards the coffee shop in search of somewhere to sit.

'Hey, Charles, let's get a hot drink.'

'I can't. I have no money.'

'It's okay. I will buy it for you.'

'But I can't pay you back.'

'You don't have to. I don't want you to.'

'Okay,' he said, grinning up at her and thinking that she must really be his friend now. No one apart from his mother ever bought him anything.'

'What drink would you like?' she asked, as they stopped by the counter and joined the queue of customers.

'Er, I would like hot chocolate, please.'

'Okay. Well, go find a seat.' Amanda scanned the area for empty seats and seeing a couple of empty armchairs at a table by the window, she pointed towards them.

'Charles, take the book and go sit at the table by the window.'

Charles took the book from her and swiftly headed over to the table.

A few minutes later, Amanda joined him, holding two paper cups of hot chocolate. Charles got down off the big black armchair and placed the book on it. He began to remove the old paper cup and the napkins that were left messily on the table.

'I'll throw these away,' he said.

'Okay. Please get some more napkins,' Amanda said, and Charles nodded in reply, heading toward the bin. A few moments later, he was back at the table. He wiped the wet coffee circles dry and climbed back up into the armchair.

'You like to clean?' Amanda asked.

'No, but I have no choice at home or Mummy gets mad.'

'I don't like to either, but I guess we have to,' Amanda said, and Charles nodded in agreement.

'There's your chocolate. It's hot, so be careful,' Amanda said, pointing to the red paper cup with Nicola's printed on it.

'Thank you, Amanda. It's very nice of you.'

'You're welcome! So, let's get cracking. As you said, the quicker we get through this one, the quicker we can start the next.'

Charles handed her the book. Amanda took it and sat on the comfortable armchair.

'You know, Amanda, the only time that my custard creams are really needed I don't have any,' Charles said, picking up his hot chocolate and taking a sip.

'It's okay. So, where were we?' she asked as she flicked through the pages for the chapter where they had left off.

The two children drank their hot chocolate as Amanda read. They were a few pages from the end when Miss Carnegie approached them to say it was closing time.

'Awww, man,' Charles said, looking up at Miss Carnegie as she stood by his big armchair.

'I'm sorry, Charles, but look, everybody's nearly gone,' she replied. Charles scanned the shop and saw the last customers leaving the shop as another employee held the door open for them.

'Please, Miss Carnegie! I need to know the ending

now. I can't wait,' Charles pleaded, with his hands cupped together in front of him.

'I can't. My staff are waiting to go home, and they still need to straighten up,' she replied softly.

'I'll help you tidy,' Charles said. 'I can do it, you know. I clean at home all the time; my mum makes me.'

'Nicola, go on. Let them finish,' said a member of the staff, as he walked up to join the trio.

'Okay. But make it quick! You will both need to help with the tidying when you're done.'

'Deal,' Amanda said, and she began to read again, with Miss Carnegie standing by listening. As promised, when Amanda finished the book, they helped tidy up before they went home.

*

'That's not fair!' Charles said, much more loudly than he expected to and quickly covered his mouth.

'That's really not fair,' he said again, this time in a whisper, as Amanda closed the book as she sat on Charles's bed. They had just finished reading *To Kill a Mockingbird*. It had been two weeks since the day they spent in Nicola's book shop, finishing *Pride and Prejudice*. Even though they spent most of their time in the park, they made regular visits to Nicola's, where they would read for hours and discuss what they were reading. Sometimes when the shop was not too busy, Nicola would stop by and talk with them about what they were reading. Sometimes she even joined in the discussion.

Today they couldn't go to the book shop or the park. That morning, the rain had been coming down in heavy sheets. As soon as Amanda opened her eyes, she knew by the sound of the rain hammering against her window that the park was not an option.

Amanda got out of bed, went over to the window, and pulled back the curtain to see how bad it really was. 'We'd both catch our death walking for twenty minutes in this,' she thought moodily, looking out at the rain as it drenched the street beyond her window.

She got dressed, put *To Kill a Mockingbird* in a carrier bag, and went to meet Charles. She would ask him if he wanted to ride the bus to the shop. But when she got to the house, Charles said that he wasn't allowed out that day.

'Oh, man!' Amanda said disappointedly, throwing her hands up in the air. 'We've nearly finished this one.'

'I know, but Mum said I can't,' Charles said, looking as depressed as Amanda.

'Well, maybe tomorrow then?' Amanda said, wiping at her rain-soaked face.

'I guess so. I'll be seeing you,' he said quietly.

'I'll be seeing you,' Amanda said, raising a hand as she turned around and walked back down the path towards the gate.

'Amanda! Wait there a second,' Charles said as she turned to look at him. Then he disappeared from view, and a few moments later he returned with a big grin spread across his face. 'You can come in,' he said. Amanda's face began to brighten as she made her way back to the front door.

'But we have to be very quiet. We can't make a sound,' Charles warned, and Amanda nodded in response, her grin as big as Charles's as she stepped out of the rain and into the house.

But an hour later, Charles was no longer smiling as they reached the end of the book.

'But life isn't fair, Charles, and never will be. You just have to remember that. If anyone ever says that it is, they're lying,' Amanda said, softly.

Charles said nothing in return.

As it grew silent, Amanda began to look around the room, thinking that she'd never known a boy of his age could keep a room so tidy. It was tidier than hers; there wasn't a thing out of place. When she first entered the room, he told her to sit on the bed. She was afraid to for fear of messing up the covers that were spread over the bed with army precision. The furniture was old but well kept. The bed was up against the wall by the window. A wardrobe stood to the left of the door when you entered. There was also a chest of drawers against the wall, facing the foot of the bed. There was an old cassette tape and radio player on top of the chest of drawers, but everything else was bare. There were no teddys or action figures, no posters on the walls, not a thing to say this was his room.

'Can I put on the radio, Charles?' she asked, finally breaking the silence. Charles nodded.

'But very low and it has to stay on the station it's already on,' he said in a whisper.

Amanda got down off the bed and made her way over to the chest of drawers. As she turned on the radio, the music began to drift softly through the speakers. Amanda screwed up her face a little.

'Do you really like this music, Charles?' she said as Mozart's Requiem in D Minor, k. 626: Lacrimosa filled the room.

'I like this music very much. It relaxes me and doesn't disturb Mother like pop music does,' he replied as he moved to the window. Charles pushed the net curtain aside and stared out of the window. Amanda climbed up onto the bed and joined him. They watched the rain for a long time and listened to music. Amanda never thought she'd like this kind of music, but Charles was right. It was relaxing.

'Oh,' she said suddenly and Charles turned to her. 'Charles, I have something for you,' Amanda said, a broad smile spreading across her face.

'You are always buying me things, and I never get you anything,' Charles said, feeling ashamed as his head hung low.

'It's okay. I did not buy this one. I made it,' Amanda said as she walked over to where her jacket hung on the door handle. She pulled two friendship bracelets from it and then walked back over to the bed and sat next to Charles.

'Only girls wear those,' Charles said, looking at the two friendship bracelets she held in her hand.

'No, they don't,' Amanda said, feeling a bit disappointed. 'Besides, these are special. Look,' she said, holding the friendship bracelets up for Charles to see. One friendship band was pink with the letter C attached to it, and the other was red with the letter A on it.

'They have our initials on them. You will wear the one with my initial and I will wear the one with yours,' Amanda explained, smiling. 'Now hold out your arm,' she said, and Charles did as she asked. She tied the band around his wrist and then held out hers for him. Charles tied the pink threaded bracelet around Amanda's wrist. Charles studied the bracelet and sighed heavily.

'What's the matter, Charles? Don't you like it?'

'I like it. It's just that I never have any money to buy or give you anything,' he said, looking at the friendship bracelet and deciding it wasn't as girly as he thought it was.

'Look at me, Charles,' Amanda said softly, and Charles slowly lifted his head to meet her eyes. 'You have given me more than anyone ever has.'

'I feel like Walter Cunningham, but one day I will have lots of money, and I will buy you so much stuff,' he said with determination.

'Yes, I'm sure you will,' Amanda agreed, 'but until then you can keep giving me your friendship. Because you know you are my friend now.'

'I know. You told me that in the book shop, remember? I haven't forgotten,' he said.

'Neither have I. But Charles, you know what I didn't tell you?'

'What?'

'That you are my best friend!'

'Really!' Charles said, his whole face lighting up with this latest revelation. Charles spat into the palm of his hand and held it out to Amanda and Amanda spat in hers, and the two children sealed their friendship with 'bricks and cement.'

'You can never take this off, Charles. Not even when we are old.'

'I won't,' he said, and Amanda wrapped her arms around his waist in a hug.

Suddenly she pulled back as she heard Charles let out a little moan and flinch.

'What's wrong?'

'Nothing's wrong.'

'Are you sure?' Amanda asked. Charles nodded lightly, and the two children sat in silence for a moment.

'This is a lovely piece,' Amanda said as the music changed and Beethoven's Sonata No.8 in C minor began.

'Yes, it is. This is my favourite. It's Beethoven,' he said, then the room went silent again as they listened to the music.

Amanda stood up and held out her hand.

'Would you like to dance, Charles?' she asked, grinning.

'We can't! We'll make too much noise.'

'Not to this, we won't. Come,' she said, motioning with her outstretched hand.

Charles got down from the bed. Amanda took his hand and led him into the middle of the room. They put their hands in the formal position. As she held his waist, Charles winced and moaned in pain again.

'What's wrong?'

'Nothing.'

When Amanda lifted their hands again into a formal dancing position, Charles winced in pain again. Amanda lifted his t-shirt and saw a big purple bruise on his right side.

'M-my brother did it,' Charles said quickly. Amanda let go of him and ran out of the room.

Amanda ran down the staircase along the hall and into the living room. There she saw a heavyset black woman with a stern-looking face holding a cigarette in one hand and a can of beer in the other. Charles's mother was sitting in an armchair watching a talk show. Her head snapped around in Amanda's direction as she entered the room.

'What's with all the commotion, little girl?' Charles's mother said, through gritted teeth.

'How can you let your son beat up on Charles like that?' Amanda asked angrily.

'What are you on about?' Charles's mother asked, a confused expression on her face and annoyance in her voice.

'I'm talking about you allowing Charles's brother to beat him up like that! A month ago, he had a black eye and now his side is badly bruised,' Amanda said, glaring at the woman who was taking a puff of her cigarette.

'What are you on about? Charles doesn't have a brother!' Charles's mother snapped, as she met Amanda's glare. Then the woman's eyes narrowed as they focused on something behind Amanda. Amanda turned to see Charles standing by the living-room door with a worried look in his eyes.

Charles walked up to Amanda and reached for her hand. As Charles took it, she felt the light tremble and saw the scared look on his face. It was only then that Amanda realised who Charles's 'brother' really was. Suddenly she realised that Charles needed her just as much as she needed him. This was the reason why he stayed out of the house, come sunshine or rain! Like Amanda, he hated the person he was supposed to love more than anyone in the world.

Charles pulled Amanda from the living room and into the hallway.

'You best go,' Charles said breathlessly, as he and Amanda reached the front door.

'I'm not leaving you, Charles. You are smaller than me.'

'She is bigger than both of us and you'll only make things worse if you stay around,' Charles said, reaching for the latch and opening the door. He stared out at the torrential rain as it came down in sheets. 'I'll be fine, Amanda. Hopefully, tomorrow will be sunny, and we can go to the park,' he said.

Amanda swiped at a tear that formed in the corner of her eye.

'Don't cry, Amanda. It's okay; you did nothing wrong.'

'I did! She's mad at you, so now you'll be mad at me. I know it,' she said, worriedly.

'I could never be mad at you,' Charles said, smiling. 'You are not just my best, bestest friend in the whole world, but my only friend! Even if I had a million friends, you would still be my number one, out of all of them.'

Amanda swiped at another tear that began running down her cheek and then placed her hands on Charles's shoulders and kissed him on the forehead.

'I better be,' she whispered.

Amanda took a step forward and then stopped.

'My jacket,' she said, remembering she wasn't wearing it as she looked out at the rain.

'One minute,' Charles said and then ran upstairs.

A minute later he was back with her jacket in hand.

'There you go,' Charles said, holding the jacket out for her and Amanda took it and put it on, zipped it up and put the hood over her head.

'You promise you aren't mad.'

'I promise.'

'And you'll meet me in the park, even if it is raining?'

'I promise.'

'Okay, Charles, I'll be seeing you.'

'I'll be seeing you,' Charles said, smiling at her as he watched Amanda step reluctantly out into the rain.

As she made her way down the path, she stopped at the gate and turned to face Charles again. Amanda waited there for a long moment and then Charles gave her a big smile and held up his hand with the friendship bracelet on it. She nodded gently and pulled the gate up slightly so it wouldn't scrape. She waved to him as she pulled the gate shut, and walked down the street as Charles closed the door.

*

When Amanda woke the next morning, she got out of bed and hurried over to the window. She pulled back the curtain and smiled with relief. The sky was grey, but that was okay. It wasn't raining and, even though the ground still had a few puddles here and there, the main thing was that the heavy rain had stopped and they could reclaim the park. Amanda hurried to the door, removed the chair from under the handle, and headed for the bathroom.

An hour and a half later, she sat on 'her' swing at the park. She had been sitting there for twenty minutes when she began to get agitated.

'He should be here by now,' she whispered to herself as she looked at her watched.

Ten minutes later, Amanda had had enough of waiting and got up off the swing and made her way out of the park.

As Amanda turned onto Charles's street and began to make her way towards the house, she saw a small gathering of people outside of it. When her eyes fell on the police car and the ambulance parked outside the house,

Amanda quickened her pace. As she got near to the house, she saw a policeman leading Charles's mother to the police car in handcuffs. A few moments later, her heart sank as she saw two paramedics wheeling out a stretcher, a white sheet coving the small body that lay on it. As the paramedic wheeled the stretcher over the bumpy ground, Charles's arm dangled from it. Her eyes caught sight of the red friendship bracelet with her initial on it. She surged forward, only to be pulled back by an onlooker.

'That's my friend!' she cried out, as tears flooded her eyes.'

*

The five weeks she had spent with Charles was not just the best summer she had ever had; they were the happiest. But the day Charles died, the happy feeling died too. Amanda held on to the chain-link swing and stared at the pink friendship band with the letter C on it for a long moment.

Then she stood up on the yellow plastic base of the swing and began working the swing into a steady rhythm. As she swung back and forth, the swing cutting through the air, tears began to run down her cheeks. Not sad tears, but happy ones as she thought about what Charles said the first day they met. She hoped he was right, because as the swing picked up momentum and speed, Amanda let go. As she flew downwards and cracked her head squarely on the concrete ground, for the first time in her life, everything was right. Although she and Charles didn't live happily, they were now happier than when they had lived.

Something to Talk About

Not today! Not this time. I've had it with these little shits, Melvin Williams thought angrily to himself as he let the engine idle on the red single-decker bus that he drove. It was at times like these that Melvin hated having a wife and two children. If not for them, he would be content with living off government handouts. Although he hoped never to have to apply for job-seeker's allowance, at times he reasoned with himself that it would be less stressful than having to put up with the little shits and stupid people who boarded the W15 he drove from Hackney Central to Higham Hill each morning.

Melvin had been driving the bus for sixteen years. Fifteen years and six months of that time had not been pleasurable. Sure, it was good in the beginning. When you are earning a penny above minimum wage flipping burgers for a living, getting a call that you had a new job driving a bus around London was like getting a call from a lawyer who said a dead relative left you a comfortable sum.

Melvin's wife, Hillary, was expecting their first

child, so the offer couldn't have come at a better time. That evening, Melvin took Hillary out to a restaurant to celebrate. They ate and drank like they had just inherited a comfortable little sum, and when they got home, they celebrated like they were on a second honeymoon.

Driving the bus for the first six months was also like being on a honeymoon. The streets Melvin cruised down at twenty mph looked different. The passengers seemed to be pleasant (even by Hackney standards), the radio controller that gave out orders wasn't half as bad as the manager that was always breathing down his neck when he was flipping burgers. Hell, even the bus was clean and shiny. However, the honeymoon was over now and had been for the past fifteen years and six months.

Melvin considered himself an easy-going man who smiled easily and laughed hard most of the time. However, as he stepped aboard the bus and began punching his details into the Wayfair machine, it was like all the life and happiness that he had minutes before drained out of him. What followed was an obligatory kissing of the teeth as Melvin got ready to face the daily onslaught of passengers.

When you are driving a bus, you have to put up with a lot of crappy people. He often let things slide, even more so than the usual Jamaican man would, even though he was born in England.

Melvin put up with the elderly people who waited at the bus stop for a good while, and when the bus came, elbowed their way to the front of the line, and only then began rummaging around in their bag for their freedom pass. Most older people were slow due to age, he got that. He put up with the old ladies who got on the bus with their trolley full of shopping and gave the person sitting in 'their' seat (either of the first four seats at the front) the evil eye. Then they would sit down and pull hard, trying to wedge their trolley as close to them as possible, but still leave it blocking the walkway. In all fairness, those seats were reserved for them so, although annoying, he let it slide.

He even put up with the school kids who sat at the back of the bus, yapping away and laughing like a bunch of hyenas. Even worse were the ones who played music loudly or worse still, those who thought themselves the next Dr. Dre or Mariah Carey. They would sing, rap, or whatever they called talking fast with a lot of nonsense thrown in these days. They mumbled about how much money they 'had,' how many girls they 'did,' and how they ran their 'endz.' If they blasted out some actual Dr. Dre or some Mariah Carey, Sam Cooke, Marvin Gaye or hell, he'd even prefer some Elvis or Lionel Richie. Who didn't like the King of Cheese? He'd welcome any of that. But it was this new grime nonsense they loved. He allowed it because they were kids and kids did that. He most likely did that when he was younger himself. He couldn't remember doing it, of course, but he probably did. So, he let it pass.

He also turned a blind eye or ear to those people

who spoke so loudly on the phone that it was like they had forgotten the other person also had a phone to their ear.

He even allowed the silly woman (it was always a woman on his route) who waited for the bus to move before she stood up and started proclaiming the second coming of the Lord, the end of the world, and that we were all going to burn in hell if we didn't change our sinful ways. Melvin found it funny that the woman would say we had to give our lives to the Lord, but then later on in her speech, she'd say that our bodies were temples and that they belonged to Christ anyway. But he allowed it because everyone was entitled to freedom of speech. Even the crazies. Besides, he found the big woman with the shrill voice at times amusing, especially when a passenger had had enough and gave her a piece of their mind. Her facial expressions were classic. One of these days that tight-lipped, pursed mouth was going to open, and some unholy shit was going to slip out. Melvin was waiting for that day.

Melvin also put up with the toddlers who couldn't get their way and thought it was okay to turn on the tears and scream down the bus with their mother cooing at them to be quiet. Really, what mum should have been doing was giving the spoilt brat something to cry for.

Melvin's patience also wore thin with the person who pressed the bell repeatedly, as if once wasn't enough. He could put up with all of that. But what he wasn't going to put up with were the three little shits who tried to board his bus without their Oyster card, and got all rude when they were told to tap in. He was going to let the incident slide, but one of the little shits had the cheek to call Melvin's mother a whore when Melvin told them to come back and tap in. The little shit continued walking down the aisle towards the back of the bus and sat down.

There was no way he was letting that one slide, no matter how bad it was raining outside. And it was coming down in heavy sheets. But no one called his mother a whore and got away with it, no matter how young they were. The three little shits could drown in the downpour for all he cared. He wasn't moving that bus an inch further until all three of the boys were back outside in the rain.

'Er, sorry, but we will not be moving until the three boys who pushed past without tapping their oyster come off the bus.'

There was murmuring and deep sighs from the other passengers. Melvin sat back in his seat and watched the windscreen wipers swish back and forth, wiping away the massive drops that landed on the windscreen. Even though he had a schedule to keep, he was willing to be a minute or so late if it showed the three disrespectful lads that he meant business.

The passengers began to turn and look around for the culprits in annoyance.

'Yeah, you in the orange Adidas jacket,' Melvin said, speaking into the Tannoy and identifying the boy who insulted his mum. 'Can you and your two friends please get off the bus? There are paying passengers who need to get to work and school, and I will not be moving until you do so.'

'Come off the bus,' an elderly lady croaked. She sat in the first seat, with her brown-and-white checked shopping trolley tucked into the other seat as far as it would go and two bags of fruit resting on the empty seat beside her. Realising that the bus driver meant what he said this time, the boy in the orange Adidas jacket signalled to his two other friends, and they all got up and made their way to the front of the bus. The doors opened with a hiss and the three boys headed for the exit.

'Pussy hole!' the boy in the orange Adidas jacket shouted as he stepped off the bus and into the torrential downpour. Melvin pressed the close button, and the doors slid closed, narrowly missing the little shit's foot.

What annoyed Melvin the most about that whole situation was that these kids got their Oyster cards for free thanks to those hard-working people who paid their taxes. All these bloody kids had to do was keep the damn things in their pockets and try not to lose them.

Another thing that annoyed Melvin was that kids who had the cards used them to get on at one stop and then jump off at the next. The government wanted to moan about obesity when they were the cause. Melvin always got annoyed when he saw those news broadcasts where the government would state that it wanted to crack down on sugary sweets and fatty foods and provide more exercise for children.

'Sorry, ladies and gents,' Melvin said, and then put the bus into drive and began his journey towards Higham Hill.

There was one plus that came with driving a bus. The rear-view mirror did more for Melvin than help him see the idiots who were going to pull out of side roads and other blind spots. It helped him know what was going on inside the bus. Melvin had learned over the years that if you looked close enough, there were stories that played out in the bus while on the route from Hackney to Higham Hill each morning that could be more thrilling, joyful, or sad than anything that Steven Spielberg could put on film. Or J.K. Rowling could ever put in a book.

The weird guy who seat hopped as though he was playing musical chairs. The seat-hopper guy always seemed to turn around and give the passenger who sat behind him a look of disgust when they would cough or sneeze and did not cover their mouths.

Then there was the kid who was always running late and had to bolt it down the street towards the stop. Melvin enjoyed teasing one boy when he saw him near the bus. He'd close the doors as if he hadn't seen him and began to move off just as the boy started slapping on the side of the bus and the doors. Unlike the 'Adidas little shit,' this boy was polite and grateful to Melvin for stopping. He always thanked Melvin when he got on board, panting for breath. He thanked him again when he got off, so Melvin didn't mind waiting a little. For all Melvin knew, he could have had to do chores before leaving the house, or he might have a small part-time job after school and had to do homework till all hours of the night. Of course, he could have been up playing on his computer until the early hours, but that was beside the point. He was a polite kid and manners count. Melvin was sure that if he chose to be a professional athlete one day, he could sure give Usain Bolt a run for his money.

There was also the single mother who worked nights at the Tesco Morning Lane stacking shelves. Hers was another story Melvin liked to 'read.' She was often dead tired when she boarded the bus, but never failed to say good morning with a smile. As soon as she sat down, she was asleep within minutes, with her head resting against the window. She stayed that way until she reached the last stop. The first few times they reached the end of the line, Melvin would just call over the Tannoy. Once, she got up and made her way sleepily towards the front of the bus and Melvin told her she slept soundly. The woman replied, 'After stacking shelves for eight hours each night, you would too.' The two officially introduced themselves. Over the past two years, Melvin would leave his cab and walk up to Julie and call to her gently until she woke. Before she exited the bus, they always exchanged a few words about their day or their families.

While driving, Melvin would find himself glancing in the rear-view mirror, thinking to himself, who would give up that? Even though she wasn't all dolled up, she was a looker. With a bit of makeup, she would have been even more so. She had beautiful dark-brown hair, light-brown eyes, and a slim build. If he was single, he'd be on it. But he didn't need to be on anyone.

Hillary wasn't anything like Sleeping Beauty back there. Still, she was pretty enough, and even better, she was all that he needed. She was a good mother—no, a great mother. They were both on the same page when it came to raising the children. She was easier on him than his friends' wives were when he stayed out or wanted to do things other wives would give their husbands shit for. She hardly ever moaned at him and they hardly ever fought.

The only downside was that the things in the bedroom department had slowed down quite a bit. Yet she was always attending those Ann Summer parties with her best friend, Samantha (who Melvin would have sworn had the hots for him). You know, the ones where they sell undies and sex toys and play games. So no, she wasn't the hottest woman on the planet, but she was all that he needed. The only thing that Julie had on Hillary was that Julie didn't snore. Hillary denied it repeatedly, but she did. Oh boy, she did.

However, there was no harm in a bit of window shopping, so long as he didn't try it on for size. If he did, he'd be the one that would be put back on the shelf, and she'd want a refund with interest. There wasn't a chance of being shelved. He was a lucky guy, and he knew it.

Another passenger whom he watched with great interest was a white boy who always sat at the back of the bus. He always sat on the left side with his nose stuck in a book—until they got to Essex Road and a black girl about the same age got on. When this happened, his book would quickly be forgotten, and his eyes would be glued to the back of her head.

Sometimes when Melvin would look in the rear-view mirror, he would see the boy look at the girl and mumble to himself. Once he even caught the boy nod to himself, take hold of the bar, stand up, freeze, and sit back down again. Melvin understood perfectly what was happening. For the past two weeks (that's when Melvin first noticed), the schoolboy had been working on his game and, obviously, it wasn't going so well.

Over the two weeks, in between staying safe on the road, keeping his eye on who was trying to board the bus without their Oyster card, and an occasional peek at the 'sleeping beauty,' Melvin watched both the boy and girl in the rear-view mirror. He enjoyed watching how things were playing out between the two of them. He hoped that the boy would just make his move before someone else did. After all, time waited for no one. If he spent too much time procrastinating, some other smart ass with a go-getting attitude would come and snatch her up. All the while, he's there umming and ahhing, and then he'll be shoulda-coulda-wouldaing all the way home with his head hung low.

*

Ben Tucker sat at the back of the bus with his head resting against the window as the relentless downpour beat against the pane. Ben sat deep in thought as he weighed the pros and cons of what would happen if he carried out his plan.

Cons: He could be ignored badly and die of shame. She could laugh at him, and he'd die of shame. He'd go up to her, she'd smile, his mouth would dry up, he'd start to stutter, have nothing to say, and he'd die of shame. Or worst of all, she could have a boyfriend. A mean looking, Bruce Banner when he's not Bruce Banner kind of dude. The kind who crushed scrawny, blond-haired, blue-eyed boys for just looking at their girl. Let alone thinking that they had the balls to actually talk to them. And he'd die of the only thing worse than shame. Pain and lots of it.

The Pros: She didn't have a boyfriend. Or that when he walked over to her, he did it with so much swagger that he looked like the other Bruce. Bruce, the billionaire playboy, who always dressed to impress and had so much confidence that he never feared talking to hot girls. Being scared of their hulking boyfriends and dying of shame was not an option. He'd walk over to her with such finesse that when he got to her seat, she'd look up at him, flash her pearls, remove her bag, and say, 'Sit, I've been saving this for you.' He knew what he wanted to do. He knew what he should do, but the cons list outweighed the pros list four to two. The odds were heavily in favour of death of many kinds, and he was only fourteen, so he didn't want to die just yet.

As the bus turned the corner, it approached the stop where she usually got on. Ben had been thinking and dreaming about this girl for three weeks and one day. She was the most beautiful girl he had ever seen (at least for three weeks and one day). A girl whose name he did not know and because he was such a chicken shit, he would likely never know.

The bus slowed down and the doors hissed open, allowing the sound of the rain to magnify throughout the bus. Ben sat up straight and looked towards the front of the bus. He tried not to make it obvious that he was staring at the black girl of about fourteen years of age who stepped onto the bus.

'Thank you,' the girl said softly, as she tapped her Oyster card on the reader.

'Morning,' Melvin said with a smile and slight nod of the head.

'Morning,' the girl replied. She turned and walked down the aisle as the doors closed. The wind and rain become a dull thud as they hammered against the side of the bus. Ben always liked that sound when he was on the bus. It always made him feel relaxed. The sound reminded him of rainy weekends. He would relax at home on the lazy boy, wrapped in a duvet, watching Star Wars, Forrest Gump, or Pretty Woman (not that he'd ever admitted it to his friends). But at this moment, Ben couldn't hear the relaxing thud of the raindrops hammering against the sides of the bus. He wasn't feeling relaxed, not at all. The girl held onto the handlebar just beyond Melvin's cab as the bus began to move.

All Ben could hear was the heavy sound that was coming from his chest as his heart hammered against it. Ben turned slightly towards the window while keeping sight of her out of the corner of his eye. *God, she was beautiful. The way the rain had shaped her hair was…She should be on a billboard.* Although, Ben and his mother weren't ones for going to church. Apart from christenings and the odd wedding, he and his mother hadn't set foot in a church since his father died seven years ago. Nor was he one for saying a prayer, but it was at times like this that the reality of God crossed his mind. *Mere humans couldn't create something as beautiful as she was, on their own. Even when she was sporting the messy wet look. She was breathtakingly beautiful. With her hair plastered to her face, dripping wet, and her mascara running down her cheeks, she looked gothic.* Not that he had seen a black Goth girl before. But the look worked on her.

*She actually looked like Nia Long when she wore her hair—well, long. That's right, I may be white, but I'm down with black cinema…*Boyz in the Hood, Friday, Higher Learning, Menace to Society, Juice, Do the Right Thing. *I've seen them all and, come to think of it, I'm gonna do the right thing, right now. I may be four years away from officially becoming a man, but today I'm gonna act like one. Today I'm gonna get up and walk over to her and say…What?* The little voice in his head asked. *Are you going to walk up to her and say, Hey there, for the past three weeks I've been watching every film with a black person on the cover just so I can come over and speak to you?*

God, she was beautiful, he thought again, pushing the negative voice in his head away. He saw her run a hand through her rain-soaked hair and move it out of her face.

Not in his fourteen years on God's once-green earth had he ever seen someone so beautiful. No actress, singer, model, super or otherwise, looked more amazing than the girl who stood a few metres away from him right now. Six weeks ago, the love of his life was Ariana Grande. The week after that it was Khloe Kardashian, and the week after her it had been Emily Ratajkowski. But this angel standing in front of him had held the top spot for a record-breaking three weeks and one day. That was the problem, though. The fact that there was no television or computer screen between him and his dream girl made things a whole lot harder.

As the girl began making her way down the aisle towards a vacant seat, Ben's heart began to pound even harder against his chest, threatening to break through. All thoughts of him acting like a man were lost as their eyes met. *Okay, so maybe I won't act like a man and go the full one hundred,* Ben thought, as his mind began to search for a backup plan. *Maybe I'll just smile. Yeah, that's it! I'll smile. If she returns the smile, at least I'll know she's interested. If she doesn't, at least I will know and can move on. Now to let those pearly whites shine. It's always hard to smile when it's not done naturally. You end up looking like a prat,* the pessimistic voice in his head reminded him wisely.

Ben refused to take heed of that voice and turned to look at the girl, instead. He gave it his best shot and smiled. Ben's lips drew a thin line as they parted with just enough room to see a flash of teeth before his nerves took over, and the smile flopped. *I knew it! I told you,* the pessimistic voice screamed at him, as though it was alerting him to danger. The girl turned away from him as she got to an empty two-seater a few rows in front of him. She put her bag on the seat by the window and sat down in the one nearest the aisle.

Ben sighed, deeply annoyed with himself. He stared out of the window for a long time. *How is this so hard? Dad did it, and granddad did it too…They did it, why can't I?* Ben thought. Through the window, he saw a man and woman holding hands. The man was holding an umbrella with his free hand, shielding them both from the downpour.

As Ben turned his attention from the street scene and back towards the girl, he saw her fix her hair and then rummage around in her bag for something. She withdrew a compact mirror and wiped her eyes and cheeks with a tissue. Then she took out a mascara pencil and applied it to her eyelids. Putting the mascara pencil back into her bag, she took out some lip gloss and applied it to her lips. He moved slightly and caught a glimpse of her in the small, round mirror. She didn't need makeup. She was already beautiful. As the saying goes, if it's not broke, don't fix it. Then another thought dawned on him. One of the cons may turn out to be true. She did have a boyfriend, and she was getting all dolled up to impress him!! And he probably was a big, hulking, brute. A mean Deebo-looking idiot. Well, either that or she was auditioning for *Britain's Next Top Model*. Which she was going to win, obviously.

Suddenly everything in Ben's body froze as the girl turned around and looked straight at him. Their eyes met for more than a brief second. Ben didn't know how long it actually was (he was too scared to count), but it seemed like forever. Even one of his smiles would have looked a million times better than the look of fright he wore. Ben's eyes darted to the floor, avoiding any more contact. He sank lower into the seat as she turned to face forward again.

Stalker, the pessimistic voice in his head screamed. *Now she's gonna think that you're a weirdo. After all, you've been staring at her angelic face for over three weeks. Three weeks and one day, and you haven't said anything. You haven't even uttered a word. Or given her a cool nod of the head, as some guys would. Just a half-arsed, if you could even call it half-arsed, smile. Which must have put her on edge. And now she's caught you looking at her in her mirror. If she only had an inkling that you might be stalking her before, well, now she knows for sure. Now her big, mean, Deebo-looking boyfriend is going to give you a bloodied nose at best. I'd hate to be you! Oh, wait, I am.* Ben sunk even lower into his seat, not knowing where to look or what to do. Just as long as it wasn't looking straight ahead.

But wait a second. Wait just one tiny second, the

optimistic voice in his head said, taking over. *Maybe this could be a good way to introduce yourself. You could go over to her and say, 'Sorry, I didn't mean to stare, but you look so beautiful that I couldn't help it.'*

Ben's spirits brightened for a moment, until Mr. Pessimistic decided to voice his opinion.

Really? You're gonna say that? Why not just go up to her and say 'Did it hurt…The fall from heaven? Or even worse, you could give her the old, 'Do you know why the weather is so shit right now? Because God is letting his wrath rip over the land because he's realised he's missing an angel.' Go on. You do that and see how far you get. You listen to that idiot, and the only thing that's going to happen is that she's gonna laugh in your face and think you the biggest idiot ever to walk the face of the earth.

Ben sighed once more, and his head automatically flopped to the side against the window. *No, Ben, you do it! It's better to say something and be laughed at than sit here wondering forever and ever,* Mr. Optimistic countered. *And also what you are saying is true, so don't listen to that old sourpuss. You take his advice far too much and where has it gotten you? The back of the bus, alone. If you take my advice, come Friday evening you could be in the back row of an auditorium not watching a movie, if you get my meaning.*

Ben smiled a genuine smile of hope. A smile so warm that if the girl was looking his way right then, she might have smiled in return.

Wow, did I just see a pig fly past the window?

Oh, just shut it.

Fine, dumb ass, you go make a fool out of yourself.

Ben lingered for only a brief moment, then took hold of the pole on the seat in front of him and began to get to his feet. Suddenly the bus screeched to a halt, and Ben let out a yelp of pain as his face smashed into the pole. He sat back down and began rubbing the side of his face.

The bus began to move again as Ben finished soothing his face. He looked up to see a load of school kids had boarded the bus. Looking in the direction where the girl sat, he noticed a tall black boy in a school uniform standing beside her seat. The boy was saying something to her, and she smiled and nodded.

Next, she picked up her bag from the window seat and slid over so the boy could sit in the seat beside her. Ben watched in horror as the two talked. They stopped talking after a couple of minutes, and the girl turned towards the window and stared out onto the rainy street. Moments later, the boy said something else and she turned back to listen to him. She nodded, then turned to look in Ben's direction. Then she turned back and looked at the boy with a straight face as he continued talking.

Oh God! I was right! That's her boyfriend! Okay, so he may not be a mean-looking Deebo, but there's no doubt that he can kick my ass. I'm getting off! I don't care if I'm four stops away from my destination, and it's raining cats and dogs. I'd rather get a little bit wet or have the flu in the morning than a black eye or two.

Ben stood up and began to make his way down

the aisle towards the front of the bus, taking hold of each pole as he walked so that he could keep upright on his shaking legs. His mind was focused on getting past where the girl and boy sat. What if she was telling her boyfriend about catching Ben looking at her in the mirror? Her boyfriend might want to go after him. Ben had a plan, though. He could run for the doors and press the emergency exit button.

Ben sighed with relief as he made it past them. He looked back as he reached the driver's cab just to make sure he was in the clear. As he saw the boy still talking and the girl still listening, his nerves began to calm, and the slight tremble in his legs slowed.

As the bus slowed to a stop, causing a little wave of rainwater to splash up onto the pavement, the doors opened.

'Goodbye. Have a good day,' Ben said to Melvin as he passed the driver's cab.

'Yes, nice one, bless,' Melvin said, nodding to Ben and Ben exited the bus.

Ben stood in the rain for a moment as he watched the red single-decker bus drive off into the distance. His heart sank with the realization that now there was no chance with her. As thunder rumbled overhead, Ben looked up. Lightning flashed, illuminating the gloomy sky for a moment, and then as the sky darkened again, Ben began to walk.

We probably wouldn't have anything to talk about anyway.

*

Rebecca Chandler's footsteps sounded more like those of a baby elephant than those of a slim fourteen-year-old. Her shoulder-length hair bounced up and down with every thump, her deep-brown eyes fixed on the front door. Rebecca picked up the umbrella resting underneath the coat rack and made a grab for the door latch as her father's deep voice called out from the kitchen and carried into the hall.

'Come back here and get something hot down you, before you leave.'

'Not hungry, Dad. Gonna be late,' Rebecca called out, as she pulled the latch and opened the door a few inches.

'Now!' Her father's voice filled the hallway once again.

Rebecca sighed, closed the door, and hurried down the hall and turned into the kitchen.

'Morning, Becca,' her father said as he put down his coffee cup and picked up a slice of buttered toast.

'Morning, Father,' Rebecca replied. She took the slice of toast out of her father's hands and took two quick bites.

'Hey, that's mine! Yours is over there,' he complained as he pointed at the toast and tea that sat across from him.

'The other person's always tastes better,' she replied as she put the half-eaten toast back into his hand and picked up his coffee cup and took a big gulp.

'God, Father, you should really start drinking tea. You know I hate this stuff,' she said.

'That's why I made you tea over there.' Her father sighed, pointing a finger in the direction of the untouched tea and toast.

'Right, Father, I'm off. Gonna be late,' she said as she bent down to give her father a kiss on the cheek.

'Love you,' she said and then turned and hurried over to the door.

'Becca!' her father called as he got up from his chair.

'How do I look?' he asked, straightening his tie. Rebecca turned and said what her mother had said for nineteen years, and what Rebecca had been saying for the past eight months.

'Impeccably dapper and ready to win.'

'You, too,' he said and blew her a kiss.

Rebecca closed the front door and hurried down the path and out of the garden. With her mind on getting to the bus stop on time, Rebecca set off at a sprint. Rainwater splashed around her as she ran down the road towards the bus stop. She stopped at a side road and in the distance, she saw the bus coming up the street, the windscreen wipers swishing back and forth. She looked down at her umbrella, only then remembering she had it in her hand. She crossed the road quickly and broke into a run.

As she neared the stop, Rebecca slowed to a walk. As the bus neared the stop, Rebecca took a step back to avoid the small wave of water that splashed up onto the pavement. The doors opened as Rebecca took out her Oyster card and boarded the bus.

'Thank you,' Rebecca said, as she tapped her card against the reader, causing the machine to bleep twice. Melvin nodded and smiled at her as she turned into the aisle. She took hold of the bar that was just beyond the drivers' cab. And there he was, sitting at the back of the bus in his spot by the window.

She knew he would be. After all, he had been doing so for the past three weeks. Rebecca pretended to scan the bus for an empty seat while looking over at him and checking him out. *God, I must look a mess*, Rebecca thought, then ran a hand through her rain-soaked hair. She made her way slowly down the aisle, looking at him, willing him to look back at her when suddenly their eyes met for a brief moment. *Was that a smile?* she wondered. She got to a completely vacant seat and saw the boy's mouth move ever so slightly. Becca sighed inwardly, wishing it was. At least then she'd know, and she would be able to smile back or nod in response. She'd feel really stupid smiling at someone and not have them smile back. *I mean, what if that little facial expression just then was him mocking me because of my wet hair and runny mascara?* Rebecca's face stiffened in disappointment, and she turned into the vacant seat next to her and sat down.

Rebecca sat motionless for a second, her brain working overtime. *Maybe I should do it. I've been trying to make eye contact with him for three weeks and one day. What's stopping him from saying hi? He's probably just shy. Every time I look his way, he turns to face the window or starts looking on the floor for something that he'll never find, and then his eyes dart back towards the window. That's it. I'm going to do it. At least then I'll know. I'll just make eye contact and nod. If he returns the gesture, maybe I'll get up and go sit next to him,* she thought, trying to talk herself into it. She brought her hand up from her side a little as though reaching for the pole, but then reached for her bag instead. *I'll do it, but not looking like this.*

Rebecca opened up her backpack and took out her makeup compact and some tissue. She wiped the running mascara from around her eyes and cheeks. Next, she applied more with her mascara pencil, then some fresh blush. Rebecca began rummaging around in her backpack again and pulled out some lip gloss. Examining herself in the mirror, she thought she could look a whole lot worse.

Through the mirror, she saw the boy looking right at her. *Right! I'm gonna do it!* Rebecca turned and was about to smile, but as she did so, the boy's eyes hit the floor. Rebecca turned back around, sighing heavily.

She looked in the mirror one more time and saw the boy taking hold of the bar in front of him and stand up. *This isn't his stop,* she thought. *He must be coming over to speak to me. Finally*! Rebecca sat up straight, running her hand over her hair one last time. Suddenly the bus screeched to a halt, and she heard a loud moan come from behind her. Rebecca turned to see the boy holding his head. *Now! Now is your chance! Get up and say something, anything. Are you okay? Would be a good start and perfect in this situation.*

Come on, just do it. You're an even bigger chicken than he is. Come on! Rebecca turned to get up from her chair.

'What's up?' said a voice from beside her seat, and Rebecca looked up to see Raymond Rogers standing beside her. Rebecca didn't know Raymond, but she certainly knew of him. Raymond had been following her around since the start of the school year. Stalking would be the more correct term to use.

Wherever she went, he was there. In the lunch hall, the library, and hallways. He was there watching from afar, so much so that when she saw him staring at her from across the way, she would say to herself, *there's that guy from my favourite horror movie again. Well, at least he's not wearing a pair of overalls and a white mask or holding a big-arse kitchen knife.*

To be honest, she'd prefer him to be wearing that combination rather than what he was wearing now.

He had on a big puffy jacket with a huge furry hood. Underneath the hood, he wore a woolly hat which sat on top of a cap. His school trousers were so baggy. Even though they were covered by the huge coat and the fact that it was pouring with rain, she knew that he was wearing them halfway around his backside. Who does that with school trousers? She could at least try to understand when they did it with jeans and tracksuit bottoms, but school trousers? What was the point? When he got to school, he'd have to fix them right anyway or face detention. She laughed to herself at the thought of bringing him home to meet her father. *He'd freak out. Sorry mate, this isn't going anywhere.*

'I'm Raymond. We go to school together. We're in the same year,' Raymond said.

'Yeah, I know. I've seen you around.'

'Really? Cool!' Raymond said a little too enthusiastically.

I said I saw you around. I didn't say I stalked you too, Rebecca thought. 'I'm Rebecca,' she said, forcing a smile.

Then there was silence, the most awkward silence, as Raymond racked his brain for something to say. Rebecca turned around to look in the boy's direction, wishing it was him she was sitting next to. She turned back as Raymond finally began to speak again.

'So, er, Rebecca, I was wondering i-if you'd like to go out sometime. We can go see a movie or just hang out?' he bumbled nervously.

'I can't, sorry, I have stuff to do.'

'Maybe next weekend then,' he asked with a little hope.

'No,' she said quietly but firmly. She said it just loud enough, so only he could hear. She had noticed a few of his friends near the front of the bus were watching them.

'Oh,' Raymond said as the hope faded from his eyes. Raymond searched the bus, trying to look anywhere but in the direction of his friends. Failing to do so, he looked straight ahead, and he caught a glimpse of his friends watching. Smiling, he turned back to Rebecca and nodded.

Rebecca's eyes drifted towards the aisle as she caught a glimpse of the boy's brown Super Dry raincoat and his Nike backpack. *This isn't his stop. Where's he going? Why is he getting off now? He still has a few more stops to go?* She was annoyed that she didn't get up and make her move when she had the chance. *Call out to him! Say something. Say anything.* She didn't, and it was too late. The doors opened with that familiar hissing sound, and the boy stepped off the bus into the rain. As the bus drove off, Rebecca slumped her head against the window. She thought to herself, *we probably had nothing to talk about anyway.*

*

Melvin sat inside the cinema foyer. On the table in front of him sat a large bag of warm untouched popcorn, and a large Pepsi, also untouched. Melvin never saw the sense in buying a different size of either. The small and medium were far too small to be spending what they cost these days. Usually, when he came on his own or with his wife, he would finish the drink on his way home and take the popcorn for the kids.

He sat in the foyer waiting for his screen to be ready, staring at his paper ticket for *Back to the Future*, but not really seeing it. His mind was not on the thought of how exciting it was going to be to see his favourite movie on the big screen for the first time ever. He was wondering whether he should have bought the ticket at all.

Melvin had finally got to see his wife in some of the sexy lingerie she had been spending her money on. And the reason why she was spending a lot of time at those parties that flogged their gear like they were selling bloody Tupperware. However, instead of plastic storage boxes, they featured skimpy undies and other accessories to be used in the privacy of your bedroom. Melvin didn't mind, of course. It was all a bit of harmless fun. And let's be honest, even though she got to wear the lingerie, it was really for him. So, of course, he didn't mind her spending money on those things; he'd be reaping the benefits, or so he'd believed.

Melvin had finished work a little earlier than usual that day. As he walked up the steps to his front door, his eyes caught sight of someone in the window. It was his wife in some red-and-black lingerie bra and thong, standing in front of the mirror. The grin that spread across Melvin's face was like he had just won the lottery. Jackpot, baby. His mind was running wild as he saw his wife through the window. It had been a long time since he was allowed access to the goods (not that he had done anything wrong to be denied them in the first place). But it seemed like the candy shop was back open for business, and boy, oh boy, was he ready to take a tour! *But, baby, you should have closed the curtains all the way. You don't want everyone and their mother to see. That view should only be for… obviously not me!* Suddenly another sexy figure came into view, wearing a black silk robe. It was Samantha, her best friend.

Melvin's chin hit the floor as Samantha began kissing Hillary's neck. She turned Hillary around to face her and Melvin's eyes nearly popped out of his head. Samantha and Hillary began some heavy lip action. Hillary pulled at the lace that was tied around the robe. As it came loose, she slipped her hands through it, briefly caressing Samantha's breast before working her hands up to her shoulders and removing it from around Samantha's shoulders. Hillary smiled that dimpled smile of hers that made him always give in. He saw it didn't only work on him, because that cute and playful smile that made Melvin lose it also seemed to have the same effect on Samantha. The black silk robe was quickly lost to the floor, and Samantha stood there completely naked as they began to go at it.

It was like a scene from one of those films that he sometimes watched, but would claim when asked that he stopped watching them long ago. But it seemed she watched them too, and even more than he did. It looked like a scene from a film that he would have titled, 'Girls Gone Wild' and then, 'Way over the Top.'

The curtains weren't open all the way. To be honest, they weren't opened much at all. However, if a pizza delivery guy came to deliver dinner, he would have gotten the greatest eyeful a man could ever want. The scene was out of a porno movie, the feeling, however, wasn't. Melvin, and maybe every other man who had seen this scenario played out in a porn movie, instantly thought, *I wish that would happen to me.* It would be a happy feeling because he could walk in and catch them in the act. At first, the two women would act all bashful, but then they would invite him to join them, and they would all live happily ever after in threesome heaven. He'd be the envy of all his mates.

However, he didn't feel excited in any way. The smile that spread across his face had faded, and there certainly wasn't anything happening in the lower regions anymore. He was numb. He felt nothing as he stood on the third of the six steps that led up to his front door and watched the scene. If it was on a television or computer screen, it would have been one of the best scenes ever.

After what seemed like an eternity, Melvin finally turned around and walked back down the steps, and away from the scene that he'd never truly get away from.

Melvin stopped when he was a few houses down the street. He thought maybe he should go back and have a good talk with both of them. Then thought better of it. The conversation had been drying up as of late. Even in the beginning, when Hillary didn't want to talk, you would get more out of a brick wall. He would talk to her when he had calmed down and thought of what he was going to say, instead of just blowing a fuse. Not that there was much to say in light of what just happened. That was as plain as day. There were many things to be said about the issues surrounding it, but there wasn't anything to say about what he just saw. Nothing to say at all.

So, there he sat, staring at the ticket and thinking. For nearly twenty years, the life he thought he had was a sham. At least he knew now that those long glances that Samantha used to send his way were those of envy, and not of lust. As Melvin thought about all the stories he had watched that day, and then his own story at home, he laughed at the complexity of the human race. Humans were funny creatures. He would have never seen it, if he hadn't seen it.

'Excuse me, Melvin?'

Melvin jerked his head up in the direction of the voice. He was surprised to see Julie standing in front of him. She had a drink in one hand and her jean jacket in her other.

Melvin's breath caught in his throat, and the voice in his head screamed, *I knew it.* Her cheeks were lightly covered with some blusher, making her cheeks glow in just the right way. She had a little red eye makeup on, making her light-brown eyes almost shine.

'Hello,' Melvin said, surprised to see her standing in front of him. What a sight to behold after the time he'd been having. 'It's a surprise to see you here. Shouldn't you be sleeping?' he replied, after a short pause.

'Yeah, I should be, but I don't sleep all that well.'

'You mean unless you're on a bus?'

'Yes,' she laughed lightly. 'You know I have a two-year-old, and as soon as I get home, I'm up with him. I do catch a few z's when he's napping, but I'm used to it,' Julie said, smiling easily.

'So where is he now?'

'He's at my mum's house. *Back to the Future* is one of my favourite movies and the only untouched trilogy left. I mean, don't get me wrong. I love Indiana Jones and Star Wars, but Lucas just won't leave those bad boys alone.

She loves Star Wars, Indiana Jones, and Back to the Future, where's the pastor…Remember, Mel, you may be heading for divorce city, but you're not there yet.

Smiling broadly, Melvin turned his ticket around and lifted it up so Julie could read the title printed on it.

'Nice.'

'It's my first time seeing it at the cinema.'

'Are you waiting for anyone?' she asked, eyeing the large popcorn and the bucket-size Pepsi that sat on the table next to him.

'No, it's just me.'

'Mind if I sit with you?'

'I insist on it.'

'Well, shall we go in? I think the screen is ready,' she said, smiling. Melvin stood up and picked up his popcorn and drink.

They began to walk towards the usher who stood by the auditorium doors, and they handed him their tickets.

'Sit anywhere you like and enjoy the movie.'

'Thank you,' Julie and Melvin both said at the same time. The usher smiled and nodded as they passed him.

'Thank you,' Melvin said as Julie held the door open for him.

'Hey, you wanna share some of this popcorn with me? I hardly ever finish it.'

'Sure, but why do you get such a big bag if you can't finish it?' Julie asked as he walked through the opened door.

'Value for money,' he replied.

'Fair enough,' Julie laughed as the door swung shut.

*

The wet gravel crunched beneath the soles of Ben's school shoes as he made his way through a nearly deserted cemetery. He was carrying a small bunch of mixed flowers.

The rain had let up, but the sky was still overcast. A light breeze blew every now and then. Ben didn't mind, though. When the day was grey, there were fewer people about, and that suited him just fine. For the past two years, whenever things got him down, he came here. Ben walked towards his father's grave, thinking about what happened on the bus that morning. There was nothing more symbolic about a boy's dreams gone wrong than a bus to crush them. Every time he replayed the scene in his head, it was like being hit by a bus. Not that Ben knew what it felt like to be hit by a bus, but that's what the embarrassment of this morning felt like.

As Ben stepped off the gravel and onto the grass, he finally focused on where he was going, instead of using his instincts. He couldn't believe what he saw. Standing two gravesites away from his father's was the girl.

He had been given another chance, and this time he was going to take it. He wasn't going to chicken out. This time he was going to act like a man. But then he remembered the boyfriend on the bus. Ben took a step towards his father's grave. As a light breeze blew across him, he unwillingly changed course and began walking in the girl's direction. No matter how hard his legs were shaking, and his heart was pumping, Ben kept on moving. Suddenly that little voice began to speak to him. For once, Mr. Pessimistic had nothing to say. *Listen, Benny boy, if she has a boyfriend, for now, it's good; that means you have no fear of rejection because there is nothing to fear. Just go up to her and introduce yourself, that's the only way you're going to find out if she's as pretty as she looks.*

Before Ben could stop himself or before he could summon Mr. Pessimistic to change his mind, Ben was a foot from her.

'Hello,' he said with confidence.

The girl turned and looked at him and smiled. 'Hello.'

'We ride the bus to school together every day. I just wanted to come over and introduce myself. I'm Ben,' he said, holding out his hand.

'I know, I've seen you, I'm Rebecca, but you can

call me Becca,' she said, taking his hand in hers and shaking it. 'It's nice to finally meet you and put a name to the face.'

'Likewise,' Ben said, returning the smile. His eyes wandered over to the headstone with a wooden cross and a gold-coloured plaque.

Natasha Leigh Chandler

Sunrise twenty-first July nineteen seventy-five

Sunset twenty-ninth August two
thousand and seventeen.

'I'm sorry to hear that,' Ben said softly, looking up at her.

'Thanks. It really sucks. You know how most people favour one parent over the other? I never did, and now I'm missing one half of my favourite team.'

'That's really sad. But you wanna know what's even worse?'

'What?'

Ben pointed towards a black marble headstone. Together they walked over to the other headstone, and Rebecca read the inscription.

George Alfred Tucker,

Loving husband and father

Nineteen sixty-nine to two thousand and seven

'You were five?!' Rebecca said, feeling shocked. 'You barely knew him.'

'Yeah, I guess. I knew him a little. I remember that we used to go to the park and play football. And we would watch Disney movies together every Sunday. But I don't remember much else. He used to smoke a lot, cigars, too. The worst kind, which, of course, was his downfall.'

'Cancer, too?' Rebecca asked, and Ben nodded slowly. 'Do you get along with your mother?'

'Yes, she's great. Well, she moans a lot, but that's what mothers do, right?'

'Yes,' Rebecca laughed, 'but you know my father always says, "Don't be bothered about me moaning at you. It should start bothering you when I don't because when I stop, it means I've given up."'

'I never looked at it that way before, but he's right. One second, please?' Rebecca nodded, and Ben walked over to his father's headstone and crouched down. He replaced the old flowers with the fresh bouquet he'd brought. He stayed there for a few long moments, said a few words, and then walked back to Rebecca.

'Have you seen *Forrest Gump*?' she asked.

'Yes, I have. Many times.'

'Well, you know that that famous quote about life and chocolates?'

'Yeah, of course,' Ben said, smiling. He forced himself not to do that famous impression that everybody fails to do right.

'Well, although they weren't completely right, they

weren't completely wrong, either. Life is like a box of chocolates, neither of the two last long enough.'

There was a long silence as he thought about what she said. He could tell she was brilliant.

'You okay?' Rebecca asked, breaking his train of thought.

'Yes, I was just thinking about what you said. It's true. They aren't. One minute you're here and the next minute you're gone.' Ben looked at her dead on and smiled. Not the barely half-arsed smile that he'd given her on the bus that morning, but a genuine smile that started off small and grew until it included a full set of teeth.

'What?' Rebecca asked, also smiling. She liked it when people could smile easily like he did.

'Life is like chocolate and full of many different flavours. Some sweet and some bitter, some smooth and some as horrid and bumpy as nuts. But if we are cool enough to take the rough with the smooth, we'll get by just fine,' he said. 'Becca, you know that boy who sat on the bus next to you today? Was he your boyfriend?' Ben asked.

'God, no. He's new to my school and has a crush on me. He has kind of been stalking me. Today he finally plucked up the courage to ask me out, but I turned him down.'

'You don't have a big, mean, Deebo-looking boyfriend, do you?'

'No, I'm not dating anyone at the moment,' Rebecca said, laughing at the way he phrased his question, thinking it was cool that he had seen the movie, *Friday*.

'Well, I was wondering if I could take you out on the weekend to see a movie?'

'I'd like that very much.'

'That's great,' Ben said, trying to play it cool. He still could not believe his luck.

'Could we sit down?' Rebecca asked.

'Yeah, sure.'

Ben and Rebecca walked over to the bench opposite their parents' graves. Ben put the old flowers into a bin next to the bench and they sat down and talked until it began to get dark. That's when they realised that they did indeed have something to talk about.

Drink

The house was in shipshape. There wasn't a thing out of place or a speck of dust that could be found. Ellie Roberts was dressed to the nines. However, she wasn't expecting guests, and she wasn't going anywhere, either. Although she was dressed in an elegant, black velvet, off-the-shoulder evening dress, it was only twelve forty-five in the afternoon. If she was going out, she'd have to take off the magenta blusher she wore to highlight her cheeks, and wipe the cherry red lipstick from her mouth, then change into a hoodie and sweatpants. Her figure was for his eyes only, and no one but him was allowed to appreciate it.

It wasn't always like this. In the beginning, there were picnics in Hyde Park and days out to the country, weekends away spent in hotels, flowers every other day, and gifts every other week.

She couldn't believe her luck when he asked her if he could see her again the night they had met. He even made sure she got to her front door safely. They met at a singles night in central London. She wasn't even there to find anybody.

She was there with her bestie, Heather, who was always complaining that no one ever wanted her. Heather had legs that went on forever and breasts to die for (and that's coming from a woman). Ellie thought Heather looked better without any makeup on than she herself did with makeup. From that evening, life couldn't have been better. Especially for someone like Ellie.

She had nothing, did nothing, was nothing. She had been born a loser. Anything she did in life never amounted to anything and why should it? Loser was in her genes. Her mother, Melanie, was sitting in the Homerton Hospital mental health unit. At times, she didn't even know who she was, let alone who her daughters were. Loser! Her father, Frank, had been sitting up in Pentonville Prison for five years of a twenty-five-year sentence. Loser! Ellie herself, who had a good education, could never find a decent job and could never spend more than six months in the mundane ones she was offered.

When Jason Baker came along, she was in between jobs, had fifty-seven pounds in her current account, and a whopping zero in her savings account. Loser! But there was Jason, the big city broker, who seemed to have unlimited funds in his bank accounts. That fifty-seven pounds in her current account and the big fat zero in her savings account didn't matter anymore.

On their second date, as they ate a steak dinner and drank wine at The Square in Mayfair, Jason said he'd take care of her. She didn't need to worry about anything, let alone money.

Two months later, she moved out of the flat in Hackney that she shared with three other people. She slept in a small room with only enough space to fit a single bed and a wardrobe. And she moved into a three-bedroom house in Islington.

Jason kept his promise. He took care of her in every way possible. He made sure she had everything she needed. But she soon learned, and should already have known, nothing is free. There is always that small print that, although you should read, you never do. All you see is the big picture, in all its splendour.

The kitchen was magnificent! Stainless-steel appliances, big cooker, double fridge-freezer, genuine granite countertops, (none of that fake stick-over shit that you can get at your local department store for a few pounds), and oak stools surrounding the island. It was all showcased by the sunlight that filled the kitchen. Through the triple bay window over the kitchen sink, Ellie had a perfect view of the neatly manicured garden.

She saw the spacious living room, with the sixty-inch television, the leather sofa and armchairs, the oak coffee table, and bookshelves filled with books on the stock market, as well as classic novels.

She saw the black Colorado fabric king-size bed, the huge wardrobe, and the bedside nightstands with reading lamps. Her bare feet sank into the plush red carpet as she walked through the house.

What she didn't see were the cleaning products stored under the sink that she'd have to use to wash and scrub the countertops, mop the floor, and polish the stainless steel.

In the splendid picture that was painted for her, she didn't see the Hoover under the stairs that rested alongside the broom. She had to use both on that plush red carpet. First, the broom to make sure all the dust and dirt were picked up properly, then the Hoover to make sure there was nothing left behind.

Ellie didn't see the dusting products she would have to use to make sure there wasn't a speck of dust on any of the surfaces around the house or a cobweb hanging from the ceiling.

She didn't see the newspaper and vinegar that she had to use once a week to clean all the windows. Ellie didn't wait to inspect the fine details of what the big picture had in store for her. Like most people, she only saw the fantastic objects and the bright colours that were shoved in her face. Six months after moving in, she'd barely be able to see the 'big picture,' let alone see the 'small print.'

Jason had invited two of his work friends over to watch the Arsenal vs. Tottenham match. However, they weren't really friends and she knew it. Even though he invited them to his house for an enjoyable evening, they still had to address him as Mr. Baker. After all, he was their superior.

If someone forgot where they stood in the scheme of things, he made sure they were quickly reminded with the Jason Baker Three Strike System.

Strike one was The Putdown. You received this

for forgetting your place in the hierarchy. Anyone who forgot where they stood by addressing Jason incorrectly, or by being late to the office, was instantly met with belittlement and mockery.

Strike two was The Shun. What Jason said went, and if you went off and did your own thing, you would instantly become the invisible man in his team and were ignored at all cost.

Strike Three was The Better Person. Anyone who Jason considered a threat to his position would quickly, for some reason or another, find himself unemployed.

Ellie laid out the hot wings, garlic bread, crisps, and other various snacks she was told to prepare on the black tablecloth that covered the oak coffee table. Jason nodded lightly at her in approval as she left the room.

She returned a few minutes later, carrying a tray with three pint glasses filled with beer. She offered each guest a drink from the tray. Jason's friends each took a pint and thanked Ellie. As she held out the tray to Jason, she saw his eyes snap up from the glass and meet hers.

'Is everything okay?' she asked.

'Yes, love, this is great stuff,' one of Jason's friends chimed in before Jason could open his mouth. 'Everything is just fine and dandy,' the other friend added, reaching for a hot wing and tearing into it, totally oblivious to the fact that the question wasn't a general one. Jason said nothing, picked up the glass from the bottom, and placed it on the coffee table.

All evening as they watched the game, she knew something was wrong, but she didn't know what. And every time she asked if everything was okay, the only answers that came were from Jason's friends. Jason said nothing at all. For most of the game, he wasn't even paying attention to what was happening on the screen.

As the game went on, the crisps in the bowls disappeared, the mountain of wings decreased, and Jason's friends emptied their beer glasses. Jason's beer sat untouched. When offered refills, his friends would gladly accept, but Jason would just shake his head, glaring at the glass.

Two hours later, she'd find out. Tottenham had lost 3-1, and the guys sat around talking about what went wrong for the team. Ellie cleared the dishes and bowls from the table and picked up Jason's friends' empties. She reached out for Jason's pint glass, but he stopped her, motioning with his hand for her to leave it where it was, not saying a word.

Twenty minutes later, she stood with him at the front door as they both said goodbye to their guests. He closed the door and walked past her back into the living room. She followed swiftly behind.

As she turned into the living room and opened her mouth to ask him what was wrong, she was only able to get the word 'what's' out of her mouth before... Wham! His fist connected with her right eye. She let out a shriek of surprise and pain as her head snapped back with the force of the blow. Her hands flew to her face. She screamed as she was struck again, not with his fist, but with the liquid from the beer that splatted in her face, adding a sting to the throbbing pain he had just caused.

'Never serve me a drink in a dirty glass again! Ever,' Jason said as she wiped the dripping beer from her face. 'And clear up this mess you caused,' he said fiercely, then walked out of the room, leaving her dazed and confused.

While she didn't have to hand over money directly, she sure had to pay for all the nice things he brought her and the things he did for her. After that night, when her eye returned to its normal state and she could see clearly again, she made sure there wasn't a smudge or fingerprint on any of the glasses and no dried-on food on any of the plates. Of course, she made a mistake now and again. And she paid for it with a slap here, a kick there, or a plate full of food to the face when something was over or undercooked. Over time, she made fewer and fewer mistakes, but the fear of another beating always kept her on her toes.

The evening after the first beating when Jason got back from work, he sent her out to the shops for some wine. When she returned, the house was in darkness. As Ellie closed the front door and turned to walk down the hall, she saw a red dinner dress hanging on the bannister that led up the stairs. She took off her trainers, put them carefully on the shoe rack, and stepped closer to the dress. There was a note pinned to it. It read 'put me on.' She took the dress and hurried upstairs and changed into it.

As she came down the stairs, she saw white rose petals leading from the bottom step through the hall, to the entrance of the dining room. She followed them as a smile of intrigue began to spread across her face. When she reached the door to the dining room, she saw a table set for two, with steaks, vegetables, and boiled potatoes, all illuminated by a single candle.

'Come and sit,' Jason said, as he stood by the table wearing a red suit with black trim around the lapel. He pulled out her chair and as Ellie sat down, Jason pushed in her chair.

'I'm sorry for what happened yesterday,' he bent down and whispered in her ear. 'I overreacted, and I was totally wrong in doing so.'

Jason stepped to the side of her. 'Truth is, Ellie, ever since the day—'

'Night,' Ellie said, correcting him.

'What?' Jason asked, confused.

'We met at night,' Ellie said as she looked up at him and smiled. She did not realise that Jason's hand had tightened around the top of the chair. He was barely holding in his frustration at her having corrected him. There was a long pause as Jason swallowed that frustration, sighed, and smiled tightly.

'Ah yes, you're right. Anyway, since we first met and for the past six months, I have fallen in love with you and continue to do so a little more each day. I can't see a life without you anymore, but I can see a long and happy future with you. So...,' Jason knelt down on one knee and pulled out a black velvet box from his pocket and lifted the lid. 'I was wondering if you saw it, too. Would you like to join me for the ride?' he asked, smiling up at her. Ellie looked long and hard into those bright eyes and then down at the white-gold diamond ring and again up at Jason and slowly began to smile and nod.

'Yes,' she said quietly.

'Finally! For a minute there I thought you were going to say no,' Jason said, relieved.

Jason took the ring from the box and held it up. Ellie held out her left hand, and as Jason slipped the ring onto the third finger on her left hand, he stood up and kissed her.

*

A year had passed since the night of the proposal. The only other ring she wore, apart from the engagement ring, was the black one around her left eye, given to her five days ago because she took too long at the shop.

Now she stood at the counter doing what she did every Saturday at twelve forty-five; making Jason's ham sandwich on whole-wheat bread for lunch. Ellie placed the second piece of bread on top of the two slices of blood-red tomatoes, pulled a big knife from its holding block, and cut the sandwich diagonally. She picked up the saucer and turned. Taking a step away from the counter, Ellie stopped and let out a prolonged sigh. She put the saucer down, pulled a white, plastic serving tray out from a cupboard and placed the saucer on top of it, tore two sheets of kitchen roll off its spool, picked up the tray, and walked out of the kitchen.

Ellie walked into the living room where Jason was sitting in a light-blue Polo shirt and navy slacks. He was reading the business news. Ellie walked up to him and placed the tray on the coffee table in front of him. Jason folded the paper and put it down on the coffee table. His eyes narrowed as he observed the tray.

'Where's my drink?'

Shit! she thought. 'I'm sorry,' she said aloud; panic beginning to rise in her. 'Be right back.'

Ellie walked over to a cupboard in the kitchen and retrieved a highball glass. Her hand was shaking ever so slightly, as she wondered what punishment she'd get for forgetting the drink.

The worst part was that the punishment never came straight away. He always made her wait and sweat it out, just like in a suspenseful movie. After the audience thought they were in the clear and could finally breathe that sigh of relief, BAM! He'd strike.

Ellie put the highball glass down on the counter and waited a few moments to steady her nerves. Then she went to the fridge and took a bottle of Coke out of the fridge and filled the glass.

'Don't forget the ice,' he called from the living room.

Ellie poured until the liquid was two inches from the top of the glass, then put the Coke back in its side door holder. She opened the freezer and retrieved the ice tray. Ellie walked over to the sink, cursing herself for making such a simple mistake as forgetting his drink. *You fucking idiot! A five-year-old would know that everyone needs something to wash their food down. When you buy a lunch deal from the supermarket, it comes with a drink. When you go to a restaurant, they offer you a drink of some kind. You've been doing this for a year and a half, you idiot. You're in for it now, and all because you couldn't remember to do what a five-year-old would. LOSER!*

Ellie turned on the tap and ran the ice cubes under the warm water for a second. She flipped the ice tray around and held it over the glass and pressed down on the first two blocks with her thumbs as the ice cubes plopped into the Coke. Three other ice cubes also came out and hit the counter and floor.

'Shit!'

'What's the matter in there?'

'Nothing, I just dropped some ice cubes. Sorry!'

'Clean it up and be quick about it,' Jason snapped back.

Ellie scrambled to pick up the ice cubes that were on the floor, wondering if this meant that there was going to be extras added to her punishment.

As she got down on her knees, she realised she was tired. Tired of everything, tired of life. Everything she did just went wrong. She thought that when she met Jason it was going to be a turning point. And it was a turning point, but not a right turn into Better Place. She took a turn at Whoop-Ass Junction and onto Shitsville.

There was no backing out and moving on because if she did, he would do what he did when she forgot to make sure a glass was clean. Or when she forgot to bring out a drink with his sandwich and a whole lot more. The thought of what he'd do if she tried to run away kept her in her place. There was no way out. Or was there?

As she began to gather up the ice cubes, something in the gap between the sink and the washing machine caught her eye. Just out of view and harm's way so you couldn't knock it over…Rat poison, sitting in a black plastic box.

*

Ellie walked into the living room with her eyes fixed on the drink. She saw nothing but the brown liquid swaying around the ice cubes as they clinked together. There was no way she was going to drop this. She kept a firm grip on the bottom of the glass to stop her hand from trembling, not with fright, but with excitement. Excitement of knowing she had the upper hand for once. That soon this would all be at an end. She'd never have to see that fucker's face again.

Sure, she'd attend the funeral and even hopefully shed a few tears (of joy), but as soon as that fucker was in the ground, she wouldn't give him another thought.

Ellie placed the drink on the tray and then sat down on the sofa beside Jason.

Jason reached for the drink but withdrew his hand

and stared hard at her as she put her feet up on the sofa. She quickly put them down on the carpet again.

Go on, make a mental note of my feet on the sofa so you can take it out on me later, along with the ice dropping on the floor and me forgetting to bring the drink out with the sandwich, Ellie thought. *Hopefully, there won't be a later. I've never seen a rat die from poison, and I doubt it will be instant. Still, hopefully, when the time comes for me to take a beating, your insides will have taken one already and you'll be too weak even to lift a finger, let alone a fist. So go on; eat, drink, and die, you fucking son of a whore. The time has come for payback, and I can't wait to see you cowering, unable to get up. Weak and helpless. Just like you watched me cower and beg you to stop. Then I'll stand and watch YOU beg for the hurting to stop. I'm gonna watch with joy as you puke your guts out. Hell, if your hair was long enough, I'd even hold it back for you. But best of all, I'm gonna watch you cry. Hopefully, you'll cry long and hard, just like I have. So, as the French say, bon voyage! Have a painful descent into hell!*

Jason reached for the remote control and switched on the television.

'In other news, Christopher Woods from Leyton in London was jailed for life yesterday after he pled guilty to killing his wife. Woods was found sitting by his bed with a gun in his hand. His wife of five years lay dead on the bed with a single gunshot to her heart.

Harry Lockhart, who lived next door to the Woods's said he broke the door down after he had heard a loud gunshot sound coming from the house. Mr Lockhart entered the house to investigate. He went upstairs and found Mr Woods sitting with his head in his hands, crying.'

'What a fucking idiot. I just don't get people like that,' Jason said, biting into his sandwich. 'Why would you want to kill anyone, especially your wife? I mean, a simple divorce would have been easier.'

'I'm sure he had his reasons,' Ellie replied.

'To shoot his wife in the heart? Come on now.'

'I can think of many reasons why someone would want to kill their spouse or partner; she could have been a patronising psycho who drove him to it,' Ellie said.

'Don't be silly, Ellie. It's not becoming of you.'

'I'm not silly. Women can do that stuff, too. There are plenty of woman like that out there. He could have been at breaking point,' Ellie said as the news coverage continued.

'Christopher Woods told the judge that he had two bullets in the gun, one for his wife and the other for himself. The second bullet misfired when it caught in the clip.'

'I'm just saying,' Ellie said quickly, as she saw Jason's eyes begin to narrow.

'It still isn't a reason for killing anyone.'

It's easy for you to say, she thought, but dared not say aloud.

'Take it from someone who knows,' Jason said. 'I was tormented in school for being fat. Now look at me,' he said, proudly patting his six pack. 'I bet you'd never had known if I hadn't told you. I could go in search of the pricks that bullied me and kick their arses, but have I? No,' he said, answering his own question. 'Why? Because I don't want to be like them.'

You should really think before you speak, you idiot, Ellie thought, trying her best to keep her cool.

'And the most annoying thing was that this fucker sat there and cried afterwards,' Jason went on.

'I guess it finally got to him and boiled over.'

'Yeah, the fact that the retard was facing life in prison. And the fact that he'd no longer get it day and night from the hottie he just shot. Look at her,' he said, referring to a picture of Mr. Woods's deceased wife that appeared on the screen. 'But he'll be getting bum-rushed in the showers every morning and in his cell every night. He's a fucking idiot.' Jason laughed, and took another bite of his sandwich.

You're the fucking idiot, you insensitive prick. Why don't you hurry up and wash down that sandwich with a little Coke. With the amount of poison I put in it, you won't need to drink it all. Not even half. So go on, you fucking waste of space. Just drink a few drops, maybe that's all you'll need.

Jason reached for the glass and wrapped his fingers around it when his mobile began to vibrate. Jason pulled his hand away, dug into his pocket, and retrieved his mobile. He grinned broadly as he read the text, until he realised that Ellie was looking at him.

'What!' he snapped, moving the phone out of her view.

'Nothing.'

'Good. Let's keep it that way.'

He thinks I don't know, but although I wasn't certain, I sure could have guessed. All the clues are there. Hiding his phone so that I can't see the message was the smallest of the clues. Always leaving the room to take calls in recent months was an even bigger one. Hardly ever being home for dinner recently was another. Yes, just the way he treated me for the first few months. Eating out was our thing. Then, suddenly, going to fancy restaurants where the chef would cook your food in front of you stopped. I became the chef. I had to cook his food to perfection or risk it being thrown in my face. Come to think about it, he didn't even take me out when he proposed. But then again, if I look on the bright side, at least I got the night off. The only time I get flowers now is after a beating. And as for weekends away...forget it. So as for his new squeeze, if it takes the heat off me and keeps him away, then she can have him...

'Hey!' Jason said, raising his voice, and Ellie jumped as it broke her thoughts.

'Huh?'

'I was talking to you! Why aren't you listening?' he said, annoyed.

'Sorry, I was just thinking you are right. The whole situation is messed up,' she lied.

'I know, right? What makes a person think they can get away with murder? I mean, clearly they don't watch any crime documentaries. If they did, they would know that you always get caught in the end.'

I mean, take your father, for example. He may not have murdered anybody. He was even lucky not to have pulled the trigger, but how dumb was he in thinking that he'd get away with robbing a bank? Especially in this day and age. What an idiot,' Jason said, eating more of his sandwich.

'Please don't talk about my father. He had his reasons. I'm not proud of what he did. But he just lost it for a moment with my mother in the hospital and him being out of work,' Ellie said, as she watched him chew his ham sandwich. *Damn, he ate as slow as a child,* she thought, as she watched his mouth going up and down.

As she studied him with pure hatred, she suddenly realised that his nose was slightly crooked. It veered to the right ever so slightly.

'Being out of work is no reason to try and rob a bank. I don't know what your father was thinking. Why do idiots like that always think they are choosing some kind of easy road? Maybe he should have thought a little longer. Then maybe he would have realised the only easy way he was taking was the easy way to prison,' Jason said, shaking his head.

Well, I guess it's as the saying goes, like father, like daughter. Because if I had thought a little longer, I wouldn't be sitting here listening to your crap, Ellie thought, as he turned away from her. Jason reached out for the drink then pulled his hand away. He looked back to her with annoyance.

'For the longest time I could have done the same,

but now look at me. I have a good job and some really good friends.'

You mean those puppets that you don't even allow to call you by your first name? The ones at your beck and call whenever you need them? You call them friends?

'I mean, not only has your dad ruined his life, but he ruined yours, too. Just be glad that I make enough money to support both of us, because who would want to employ you? They'd be too afraid they'd make the same mistake they did with your dad. You know, they do check these things. Trust me, I know,' Jason said arrogantly. 'Not everyone is as thoughtful as I was when you told me about your father. With all that I have and all the money I earn, I should have run for the hills. But I didn't and I'm glad I didn't. You may not be the hottest woman on the planet, but you are a good one,' he said, and patted her hand as though she was a child that he was trying to make feel good.

Stop chatting shit and hurry up and drink your poison, I mean, Coke. I can't wait to see you squirm. Another thing she noticed was that his eyes were much duller than she had realised. When she first met him, his eyes sparkled. But now she studied him as he chewed on his ham sandwich, talking with the food still in his mouth just like a damn child would, while staring at the television. She felt stupid to have fallen for his charm or the act of it. He was a fucking idiot who had the cash to splash and confidence that came over at the right moment for charm, but not much else. Ted Bundy was charming and look what he did…

Suddenly her eyes widened with a mix of fear and joy as Jason reached out for the glass. She bit her lip hard with anticipation as she watched out of the corner of her eye as Jason began to lift the glass. She could hear the fizzing of the bubbles as the ice cubes clinked softly together. She could see the condensation dripping slowly around his hand as he brought it slowly towards his mouth. *This is it,* she thought. *After this there will be no more belittling, no more black eyes that I have to wear exposed as I walk down the street.* She wasn't allowed to hide behind sunglasses. Jason had said that the fuckers out there had to know she was spoken for and that they'd get just what she did and more. If those boys didn't take heed of the ring around her finger, then the one around her eye should give them pause. After he downed the drink, there would be no more food shoved in her face if it wasn't cooked to his liking. After this, he'd finally be out of her life for good. She'd be free!

Or would she? She may be free of him in one way, but the son of a bitch was right. She'd be putting herself in another cage. A cage much smaller than the one she was already in, where she'd be watched twenty-four hours a day, where she'd have to share a cell with someone she may hate even more than the man sitting next to her. There'd certainly be an idiot or two who would want to give her a black eye or two. And if she murdered the fucker beside her, she'd be no better than he was. She'd be worse.

Ellie grabbed the glass just before it touched his lip.

'What the hell?' Jason said, giving her the evil eye.

'The ice cubes are a bit small,' Ellie said, thinking fast. 'It's gonna be a bit watery. Let me get you a new one,' she said smoothly. Jason's face relaxed as he allowed Ellie to take the drink.

'That's why we are good together,' he called happily, as he watched Ellie walk over to the door. Ellie ignored his comment as she left the room.

Ellie went into the kitchen and poured the drink down the drain. Putting the glass down, she gripped the edge of the basin with both hands and let out a long sigh of relief. *That was close. Really close. I don't want to be here, but I wouldn't wanna be there, either. I won't be staying here for another minute, though. I've stayed here three hundred and sixty-five days too long. The biggest mistake a man can make is taking a woman for a fool. The biggest mistake a woman can make is allowing a man to treat her like one. I'm partly to blame for not leaving any sooner, but I'm not going to be the fool for another minute.*

Ellie turned on the hot water tap and let it run until she began to see steam. She filled the glass with boiling water, then poured that down the drain. She put some washing-up liquid onto the sponge that sat in between the two taps and then scrubbed the glass thoroughly with the rough side of the sponge and rinsed away the soap. Still holding the glass, she opened the cupboard door under the sink and took out a carrier bag, tore some kitchen towel off its spool, and dried the glass. She placed the glass, sponge, and used paper towel into the bag and tied it up. She then turned back on the hot tap, squirted some hand wash onto her hands and, flinching as she felt the sting of the hot water on her hands, she began to lather up doctor-style and began to scrub.

*

'What took you—where the hell do you think you're going?' Jason asked five minutes later. Ellie walked into the living room with his fresh drink in hand and a coat over her arm. She walked over to where Jason sat, looking baffled. She put the drink down on the tray. Jason looked at the drink and suddenly noticed that floating in the brown liquid, along with the fresh ice cubes, was her engagement ring.

'What the fuck!' Jason said and began to rise, but quickly sat back down again as Ellie took her coat off her right arm, revealing a big kitchen knife which she thrust in his face.

'You crazy bitch!' he raged at her, as he tilted his head back to avoid the knife. Jason's eyes flicked back and forth as his mind ran wild, trying to think of what had come over her.

Jason made a move to get up, but Ellie placed the tip of the big kitchen knife onto his Adam's apple.

'If you don't what me to carve that in two, stay still and listen good,' she warned, her bright green eyes blazing. 'I'm going now, and I won't be back. Don't ever come looking, because if you do, I'll kill you. Is that understood?'

There was silence as she glared into her ex-fiancé's eyes. Ellie saw how petrified she must have looked all the other times she was on the receiving end of a threat or beating. She saw he was shaking slightly, and a tear ran down his right cheek.

'Don't get up,' she warned and began to back away, not taking her eyes off him until she backed out of the living-room door.

A few moments later, Jason sighed with relief as his hand went to his throat and the tears began to flow as he heard the front door open and slam shut.

Printed in Great Britain
by Amazon